Akkadian rising sun

AN ILLUSTRATED NOVEL

S. Kalyanaraman

Library of Congress Control Number 2013906117

ISBN-13: 978-0-9828971-9-5

ISBN- ISBN-10: 0982897197

Printed in the USA.

First paperback printing: 2013

Chapter 1 Kiḍāram, Khmer, Manila, Philippines and Jagadhri, Haryana

I am like a spark from Sagan's anvil in his brass foundry. Many sparks fly and vanish within fractions of a second, spark-time like the subatomic particles or like the molecules of DNA chains of life with specific functions to perform to make life form meaningful.

I am only *nimittamātram*.

Nimittam means 'instrumental or effective cause, ground reason'. There is a reason why I am given this life form.

Gitācārya Kṛṣṇa conveys the same message in his song, Bhagavadgīta 'निमित्तमात्रं भव सव्यसाचिन् *nimittamātram.bhava savyasācin* 'Arjuna, just become to be the cause for this discourse about *ātman*.

I was born in கிடாரம் கொண்டான் kiḍāram koṇḍān in Tamil Nadu but all my education was in Telugu because my father was employed as Minor Irrigation Overseer in Penukoṇḍa, Anantapuram District, the summer capital of King Kṛṣṇadevarāya. His job was to maintain the flow of water in the canals feeding the ground-nut crops of the surrounding villages. Rains were the only source of water in this District. There was no River Sarasvati nearby to assure perennial supply of water. Even for drinking water, I had to walk every morning 5 kilometers to the small lake at the foothill to fetch drinking water for the family because the water from the well was brackish, not potable and could be used only for cleaning and bathing.

As I started working in Manila, I realized that *kiḍāram koṇḍān* which is recorded in my Passport as my place of birth was so named to commemorate sea-faring cultural contacts of ancient times.

King Karikāla Cōḷa had established friendship ties with *Kiḍāram*, the Tamil form for the kingdom of Bujang valley. *Kiḍāram* was the Tamil name of Keḍah 'abode of peace' located in the northwestern part of Peninsular Malaysia. The people of Keḍah know the bounties brought by River Mekong flowing from Manasarovar glacier of Himalaya.

In the village called Piñjai, adjacent to *Kiḍāram koṇḍān*, there is a thousand-year old temple inscription which refers to the gifts given by the king to the artisans of the region. In the Singapore Kalachakra Museum, there is a model of a golden chariot which a Khmer king had given to King Karikāla Cōḷa to celebrate the Cōḷa-Khmer alliance. Khmer influence in Thai-Malay peninsula during 12th century CE is recorded by the French epigraphist George Coedes. Some historians interpret that the gift of the Khmer chariot was from Suryavarman to Rajendra Cōḷa.

Karikāla Cōḷa built a temple replica of the Brihadīśvara temple in a place called Gangaikoṇḍacōḷapuram. This Gangaikoṇḍa commemorates Karikāla Cōḷa bringing pots of water from River Ganga-Sarasvati to sanctify the waters of the temple tank. Hence, that tank is called Cōḷaganga.

Not far from the place where Khmer chariot could have been made, I visited the Viṣṇu temple of Angkor Wat in Cambodia, on the banks of River Mekong, to understand the significance of the Indian Ocean community that existed along the 63000 mile long rim of the ocean from Cape of Good Hope, South Africa to Hobart, Tasmania, Australia.

I am only *nimittamātram* as *Gitācārya* noted in another context of ancient times.

Time seems to ring the bell of memories, even as the clock keeps ticking inexorably. It is ticking, *tick tick tick*, of immortality.

I feel so proud that my place of birth brings back the reminiscences of these contacts among people established through water-bodies, be the water the salty water of the ocean or the water flowing from glacial melts irrigating fields to produce grains to feed and quench the hunger and thirst of the people.

In Karikāla Cōḷa's time, something remarkable was achieved by the engineers of yore. They created a stone anicut called *kallaṇai* and diverted the surplus waters of River Kaveri through a channel called *Koḷḷiḍam* to add another 500,000 acres of fertile land for production of rice. This *kallaṇai* model also occurs in South Africa and has led to the marvel of reborn Sarasvati using the waters of River *śutudrī* and River *vitastā* dammed at Bhakra-Nangal and Pong, gathering the waters in Harike Reservoir to make River Sarasvati flow again as a 40 ft. wide, 12 ft. deep canal into Gedra Road, Bikaner District, Rajasthan, covering a distance of over 1,000 kilometers. This model should be replicated for all rivers flowing from the Himalayas into the Indian Ocean Community to make all the rivers of this community perennial, in a water-grid for Rāṣṭram, assuring *abhyudayam*, social welfare for 2 billion people of the globe.

I told Sagan, 'I hope together with this watergrid, I will see the formation of Indian Ocean Community as a Rāṣṭram, a united community of nations along the ocean rim. With the blessings of Devi Sarasvati, everything is possible.'

Sagan agreed and went about his work in the brass foundry making his trade mark Jagadhri brass vessels

I realize that I am still a student. So, I am brought back to my religious life.

When I did my Ph.D. thesis on Development Administration in the University of Philippines, Manila, following my earlier studies in Economics and Statistics in Annamalai University, India, I documented what I had learnt about the quartet of work, decision, power and participation. Little did I realize that these were about my religious practices. I chose to make a presentation on what I had mapped as the path of River Sarasvati – from Himalayas to Arabian Sea -- in an international conference on Sanskrit studies. A strange encounter occurred which has changed my life.

I met two scholars who saw what I presented on slides. 'Hey, we are also searching for River Sarasvati. Stay in India and meet Guru,' Ravi said.

I agreed and stayed for another week so that Ravi could set up a meeting with Guru.

Guru had set up a foundation in Jodhpur, Rajasthan to organize the search.

His words still ring in my ears. 'You have to get involved. Wakankar died of heart attack and left us in the midst of our journey.'

Together we went to Regional Remote Sensing Satellite Centre of Indian Space Research Organization in Jodhpur to meet the scientists and sought their help in getting images of the path of River Sarasvati. They were aware of the Landsat images and promised to get higher resolution images using Indian Remote Sensing Satellites. It appeared reasonable to look for Sarasvati from space, after all she was a celestial, a metaphor of divinity. They kept their promise and produced a number of images stretching across Himachal Pradesh, Haryana, Punjab, Rajasthan and Gujarat.

Geologists who accompanied us said, 'we have to test the ground-truth by verifying the images on the ground'.

This took me and Guru to experts in Central Ground Water Authority of Ministry of Water Resources. They were helpful and organized a large project to dig a number of bore-wells in spots selected by Indian Space Research Organization.

The selection of the spots for bore-well operations was a class act.

The space scientists chose spots which satisfied three parameters adjacent to the spots: 1. There was a tectonic fault-line; 2. There was an archaeological site indicating ancient people living on the banks of the river; and 3. A relic water-channel was traced by satellite images. So, we have found a new class of water diviners!

Groundwater experts who dug the bore-wells reported 99% success and located gushing ground-water just 100 metres below the earth surface.

The Jodhpur foundation reported the results. Many people were skeptical and asked many questions. One legitimate question was posed by Karmi: 'OK, you have found an old river. How do you know she is Sarasvati?'

My studious religious form was shaken to reality, though I knew that an ancient rishi had referred to Sarasvati in three forms: 1. River; 2. Mother; 3. Divinity.

'Could the old channel indicated by the results be indeed River Sarasvati ?' asked Guru, again and again.

Who knows? In very ancient poems as profound as TS Eliot's 'Waste Land', she has been described as 'Mother'. She was called 'Mother', because she had nurtured a civilization on her banks. My mother had told me that there was a confluence of Sarasvati, Yamuna and Ganga in Prayag, where every 12 years a great festivity pilgrimage occurs. This year, 2013, about 50 million pilgrims are expected to take a dip in the river confluence, remembering the 'Mother' who had supported our ancestors. Like the Danube, like the Ganga, Brahmaputra, Sarasvati was the very life-force. How to identify her now, using scientific advances and proofs demanded by secular enquirers? If Brahm river had existed prior to the formation of Himalaya, did Himalaya tear asunder Brahmaputra, son of Brahman and Brahmaputri, daughter of Brahman (also called Sarasvati) – one flowing east and the other flowing west?

One poet had called her *vāgāmbhṛṇī.* From my Indian language lexicon work, I could surmise that this compound word indicated *vāk* and *ambhas*, meaning 'utterance' and 'water' – like the tears of the eyes. Was the poet using a divine metaphor of a flow of thought expressed as utterances which stand the test of time, as tears flowed down my eyes?

She was *ṛṇī.* We all owe a debt to her. She is the cause of our lives. She is the *śakti,* the primordial energy of our lives and of everything in the Universe, infinity.

I was crying, tearlessly, silently as Guru went into meditation, in a yogic state. Will the 'Mother' incarnate and appear before our eyes as a flowing stream, carrying molten snows from that great divinity of a mountain range stretching from Tehran to Hanoi?

We realized that we cannot understand the Mother unless we understood the evolutionary history of Himalayas. This inevitably took us to Keshav who has trekked on the Himalayas almost every year, year after year. When we met him, he told me and Haribhau who had taken over the mantle of the foundation from Guru: 'Himalayas are dynamic'. Browsing through his scientific writings as we sat with him, we could realize that the Indian plate is moving in a continental drift at a majestic walk of 6 cms. per year northwards. Like *varāha* the plate was also jutting into and lifting up the Eurasian plate about 1 cm. every year. Some experts claimed that *Sāgarmātā* Mt. Everest was overtaken by Karakoram K2 in Pamir plateau as the tallest mountain on the globe because of the ongoing, dynamic uplift referred to as the impact of plate tectonics. As we were enthralled, Keṣhav continued: 'The Great Thar desert has marched eastwards over 1500 kilometers, during the last 8000 years.' This hit us like a thunderbolt, like the thunder of Ganga which repeated: *da, da, da.*

Did the march of the desert engulf the channels of River Sarasvati? Did the inexorable march of the Indian plate twist the channels around resulting in the tributary *śutudrī* taking a steep turn away from River Sarasvati to join River Beas en route to River Sindhu?

Haribhau and I realized that we have to go to Darshan Lal Jain of Jagadhri who has set up a girls' high school. The school has a permanent exhibition showing satellite images of channels of River Sarsvati from Himalayas to the Arabian Sea near Somnath, Gujarat. Darshan Lal asked us to come to Jagadhri on the Full Moon day of Kartika month. That day was the birthday of Sarasvati. About

500,000 pilgrims go to nearby Som Sarovar, year after year, on that sacred day, to take a vow, a holy dip in that lake to expiate the debts they owed to their ancestors, their teachers. The pilgrims have an amazing calendar memory. They wait for the day, the way they wait for 12 years to arrive at the day of Kumbha Mela which celebrates the coming together in *sangam* 'confluence' of Sarasvati, Yamuna and Ganga.

This is a remarkable tradition, the discharge of debts, called *ṛṇamochan mela*, life itself is a process continuum to discharge debts accumulated over several life-forms.

On that day, Darshan Lal took us to another nearby lake called Sarasvati Sarovar in Adh Badri. This lake was filled with water accumulated across eleven check-dams from the glacial spring waters and also from Somb river emanating from the Siwalik ranges or perhaps, even beyond from the glaciers of the Himalayan heights, towering higher than 8000 ft. height of Siwaliks The snow and ice keep accumulating above 8000 ft. height as monsoon waters are gathered and stored to create the greatest water reservoir of the world, We prayed to the Himalaya Divinity and took a sacred dip in the chill waters of Sarasvati Sarovar which is located on the banks of Somb River.

Glaciologist Mohan was thrilled by the terraces on the banks of Somb River and asked for rock samples from the terraces. He thundered: 'This is the spot where Himalayan Sarasvati enters visibly into the plains of Adh Badri. I have found here metamorphic rocks which can come only from the bowels of the Himalayan hot-springs'

On the way back from Adh Badri to Jagadhri, we met Sagan Muṇḍa who was a brazier. He was making brass vessels alloying copper and zinc. He called it his ancestral heritage.

Sagan Muṇḍa and his wife Karmi Hatu told us how their suffering and gloom get cleared by praying to River Sarasvati and by remembering the legacy, their roots.

Sagan said: 'My ancestors were sea-faring artisans and merchants to regions beyond River Sindhu. My work unites River Sindhu and River Sarasvati.'

The profundity of Sagan's summing-up has been a cornerstone of all my education every since that day of our meeting with Sagan Muṇḍa and Karmi Hatu. How can I ever forget the taste of the tea both of them served us, announcing: 'This is Assam tea with lemon juice'. I like my Darjeeling tea with a twist of lemon juice.

The search for Sarasvati has taken many twists and turns, not unlike her meandering streams and lakes skirting the Thar desert.

Flowing waters have entered our *ātman*, the very core of our being transforming us into our becoming.

Chapter 2 Penn Museum, USA and accumulation of Indus corpora

Recollecting the account of Sagan and Karmi Hatu, I visited the artifacts kept in the Penn Museum of University of Pennsylvania.

It was spring. It was a sunny day of June 10, 2004.

Gregory Parker, Professor of Archaeology in University of Pennsylvania, told us how he walked into the Metropolitan Museum of Art in New York to participate in the 'First Cities' show.

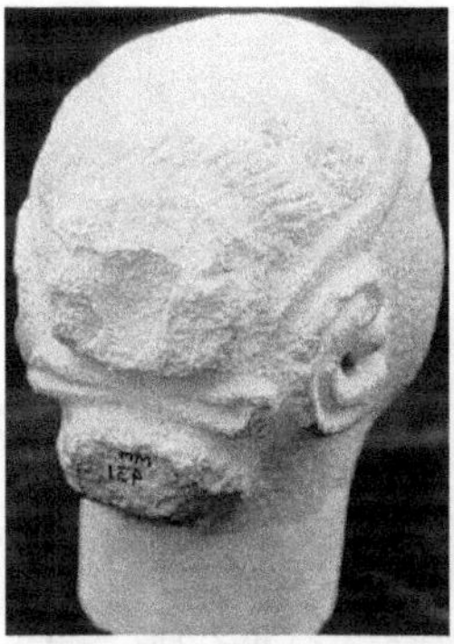

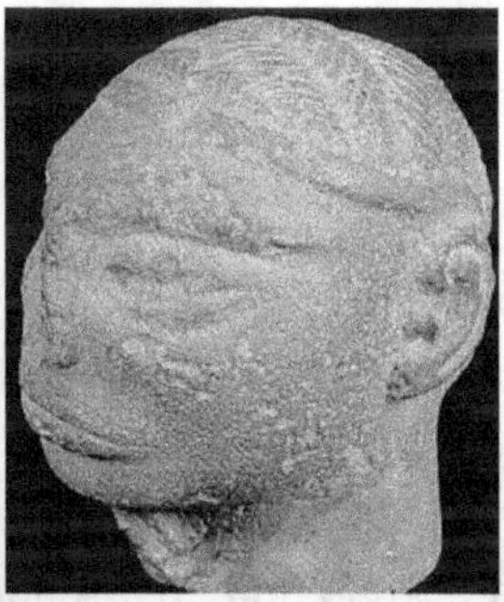

There was a sculpture of a man with finely braided or wavy combed hair tied into a double bun on the back of the head. A plain fillet or headband with two hanging ribbons falling down the back The upper lip is shaved and a closely cropped and combed beard lines the pronounced lower jaw. Long eyebrows frame the stylized almond shaped eyes. Will we ever know the name of this man?

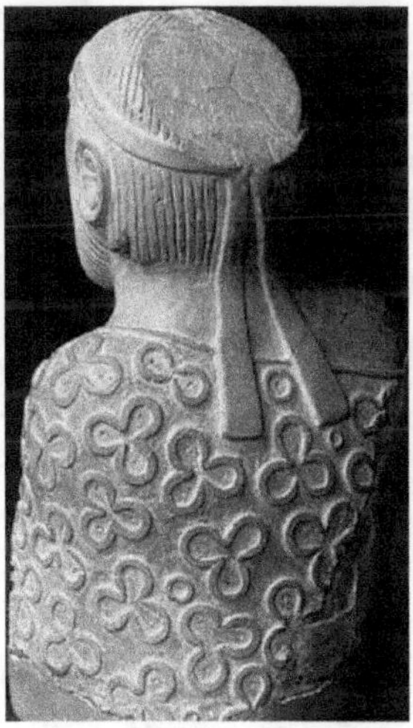

The show was a display of 3rd millennium treasures from the 'First cities' of Near East and India.

One of the galleries of the show was called 'Priest-King', statue of an old man with a trimmed beard, wearing perhaps a golden fillet on his forehead. His shoulder was draped in a shawl decorated with tre-foil designs embedded with red paint.

Blackbuck antelope and trefoil designs (like the designs shown on shawl worn by the 'priest-king') on a dish or lid with perforation at edge for attaching to a large jar. Maybe, the trefoil denoted an 'ancestor' or someone to be venerated?

'What was the name of this man?' Parker wondered as he moved to view another clay object in the gallery.

The object was a clay impression of a cylinder seal rolled out and brought on loan thanks to Conservateur General, Department des Antiquities Orientale at the Musée du Louvre who permitted Parker to make a fresh impression of the seal. The seal was made of green-grey schist and measured 2.9 X 1.8 cm.

The roll-out showed four men and a woman and an inscription in cuneiform script. Experts debated if the seal was of Late Akkadian period, about 2200 BCE (Before Comon Era) or Ur III period, about 2113 BCE.

The inscription could be read because cuneiform had been deciphered successfully.

The inscription in Akkadian language was translated. An epigraphist in the Babylonian section of University of Pennsylvania Museum confirmed the translation.

The inscription read: Shu-i-li-shu/eme.bal me-luh-ha: "Shu-ilishu—Meluhha interpreter."

The bearer of the seal, announced himself as a translator who translated from his native language into a foreign one (eme.bal). In this case, the foreign language was Meluhha.

One expert noted that since the owner of the seal bore a typical Old Akkadian name, he might have acquired a command of the language of Meluhha from new settlers.

Shu-ilishu was perhaps the man shown seated on the lap of bearded Akkadian merchant, since he is shown greeting the merchant with a lifted hand in salute. The salute is in the same posture shown by the Meluhha merchant carrying an antelope on his left shoulder accompanied by a woman carrying an alchemist's pot on her right hand.

Behind the Akkadian merchant were shown two large jars. Another jar was kept on a pedestal guarded by a man, kneeling behind the stool of the merchant.

The clue was the name Meluhha.

Meuhha is mentioned, sometimes transliterated as Me-lah-ha on some other cuneiform texts as a region in trade with Sumer or Akkad or Mesopotamia. Experts surmise that Meluhha was the Sumerian name for some area in the vicinity of Baluchistan or the Indus civilization. Sargon of Akkad said in one text: "(I) dismantled the cities, as far as the shore of the sea. At the wharf of Agade, I docked ships from Meluhha, ships from Magan."

A late Sargon tablet, perhaps dated to 2200 BCE refers to a man with an Akkadian name as 'the holder (?lu-dab) of a Meluhha ship.

An inscription of Gudea of Lagash (2143-2124 BCE) says: 'the Meluhhans came up from their country' to supply wood and other raw materials for the construction of the main temple of Gudea's capital.

One text of grain delivery (2057 BCE) refers to 'dub ur-lama dumu me-luh-ha': a tablet of Ur-Lama son of Meluhha.

An inventory of barley deposits (2047 BCE) cites 'l-dub e-duru me-luh-ha': the granary of the village of Meluhha or characterizes the settlement as 'e-duru ga-esh' : village of travelling merchants.

Some texts refer to mill staff in a temple in Girsu (Tello): scribes, gate-keepers, reed-weavers, carpenters, malsters, grinding-slab cutters, 'chair-bearers', boat towers or 'ugula me-luh-ha': overseer: Meluhha or 'e-duru ur-nig ku-dim': village of the silversmith Ur-nig.

Many Meluhhans or sons of Meluhha (ur-lama dumu me-luh-ha) had Sumerian names: Ur-Ishtaran, Ur-Babu, Nin-ana.

One is called 'Meluhha, son of Ur-ana-dua'. Ur-ana-dua is a Sumerian name.

One text contains a Meluhhan name. 'lu-sun-zi-da lu me-luh-ha-ke': Lu-sunzida, a man of Meluhha who remitted to Urur son of Amar-luku, 10 shekels of silver as payment for a broken tooth. Reverse of the tablet contained another text: 'lugal-iti-da mashkim ugula en-l-lu': Lugal-itida (was) the bailiff, overseer: Beli-ilu.

Were the Meluhhans sea-traders with Sumer or Akkad or Mesopotamia?

Was Sumerian Meluhha the same as Sanskrit *mleccha vācas*, 'meluhha speech'? I had read that Divinity Vāk belonged to the mlecchas.

One text read:

[ultu ......]x ti-tur-ri Ba-zaki sa pat(ZAG) harran(KASKAL) mat Me-luh-h[aki]

[From ......] ... the bridge of Baza on the edge of the road to the land Meluhha. Was the antelope carried on the left hand of Meluhha merchant an identifier, a professional calling card?

Characteristic way of identifying elamite persons is by making them carry on their hands an animal, say, a bull or an antelope. These are sculptures of Elamite merchants and an Assyrian sculpture of Gilgamesh holding a lion, from Palace of Sargon II, Khorsabad, c. 8th century BCE.

I present some images from the civilization contact region.

Two sides of a molded terracotta tablet from Harappa.

Pair of tigers/jackals:

On a seal. On a Pyxis Lid. Syria, Minet el-Beida, Tomb III; Late Bronze Age, 13th century B.C. (Musée du Louvre, Département des Antiquités Orientales). Tablet from Harappa.

Two late bronze age tin ingots from the harbor of Haifa, Israel contain glyphs used in epigraphs of Sarasvati civilization!

The picture of these two ingots was published by J.D. Muhly [New evidence for sources of and trade in bronze age tin, in: Alan D. Franklin, Jacqueline S. Olin, and Theodore A. Wertime, *The Search for Ancient Tin*, 1977,

Seminar organized by Theodore A. Wertime and held at the Smithsonian Institution and the National Bureau of Standards, Washington, D.C., March 14-15, 1977]. Muhly notes:"A long-distance tin trade is not only feasible and possible, it was an absolute necessity. Sources of tin stone or cassiterite were few and far between, and a common source must have served many widely scattered matallurgical centers. This means that the tin would have been brought to a metallurgical center utilizing a nearby source of copper. That is, copper is likely to be a local product; the tin was almost always an import...The circumstances surrounding the discovery of these ingots are still rather confused, and our dating is based entirely upon the presence of engraves signs which seem to be in the Cypro-Minoan script, used on Cyprus and at Ugarit over the period 1500-1100 BCE. The ingots are made of a very pure tin, but what could they have to do with Cyprus? There is certainly no tin on Cyprus, so at best the ingots could have been transhipped from that island. How did they then find their way to Haifa? Are we dealing with a ship en route from Cyprus, perhaps to Egypt, which ran into trouble and sank off the coast of Haifa? If so, that certainly rules out Egypt as a source of tin. Ingots of tin are rare before Roman times and, in the eastern Mediterranean, unknown from any period. What the ingots do demonstrate is that metallic tin was in use during the Late Bronze Age...rather extensive use of metallic tin in the ancient eastern Mediterranean, which will probably come as a surprise to many people."

Sealing of a scribe employed by the Akkadian king Sar-kali-sarri. Water buffalo, depicted here, were brought to Mesopotamia by the Harappans.

The kneeling adorants in front of the buffaloes hold a pot overflowing with water. The bottom register shows flowing waters. These glyphs are as emphatic a writing system as the cuneiform script within the rectangular cartouche.

It was time to write a poem.

Chapter 3 Sarasvati -The Fertile land

Sarasvati thundered, 'I am the *rāstrī* meaning' I am Rāṣṭram' (a complex description of a supra union of nations)..

The thunder said

Da *datta*

Start the fire.

Dadhyañc kept on counting *pūrṇam*

Taking too long to count infinity

That infinity that Brahman

This infinity this Universe

Subtract this infinity

Yet infinity remains

The thunder said

Da *dayadhvam*

Sarasvati assumed the form of Vāk

To proclaim Dharma

Aham Rāṣṭrī

I am the Rāṣṭram

The possessor of infinity

Keep counting Dadhyañc

I accumulate and show you the path.

The thunder laughed

Da *damyata*

Earth shook

Mountains parted

Sarasvati turned east

To flow into Ganga

Plates collided

Varāha lifted up the northern plate

Āsurī Sarasvati struggled to flow out of Bata valley embrace

War began

Brothers yearned for revenge

Wealth withered

As the thunder trotted *Da Da Da*

Sarasvati started crying

Shedding sorrowful tears as the earth rumbled

Drumbeat to song of thunder.

Tears of Sarasvati

Abandoned the warring brothers

The Sun darkened covered by moon's shadow

Rats died on the abandoned riverway

It was *pralayam* deluge.

The sobbing Sarasvati

Shattered families

Tore through the mountains

For an eastward path searching for the Sun.

The thunder asked Vāk, where are you?

I can't see you in this darkness

Get me the Sun. Fire still flickers.

Datta gold. Tears for *dayadhvam*.

Elo, elelo.

Damyata boatman.

Just back from voyage

To Tigris.

Take the conch from Kīṟakkarai

Blow it hard

Till *OM* reverberates to end the war.

March together, to the tunes of this

Sarasvati song

Sing in unison for *Rāṣṭram*.

Keep the fire burning till the flame flags victory.

I am Vāk, I am the empress of liberty. Walk with me.

Till we reach the oceans of joy.

Glacier melts

Flowing avalanches

Trickles as streams

Leaf turns green

As the mountain keeps growing high

Pushed up by Varāha's tusk

Carrying the baby Earth on his shoulder

Viṣṇu smiles as Varāha digs in again.

I will flow again.

Let the march of the desert stop.

Let the sand dune get washed by the chill waters.

Let the trees start growing again

As the desert vanishes

Into the dustbin history

Leaving behind alluvium rich with nutrients

Let the trees take root

Almonds, olives, squirrels nibble

Green desert *Damyata*, train, tame, control.

Boatman, come back from Tigris

Sing with me, join in chorus make history

I am flowing again to meet the oceans.

Clap, clap, clap. *Da da da* as thunder rains

Mocking the desert of poverty.

Gritsamada sang.

River, divine, mother

He called me amma.

He is my child

I will nourish him back to health

He will grow to cherish my name

Let the festivity mela begin on the river-bed.

We visited annual festivities held on the river-bed in Rajasthan.

The local elders explained the events as commemoration of ancient rishis,

a way of discharging the debt the people of the region owed to the teachers who have taught them *dharma*.

Dharma.

This brings me back to my responsibility. I am overwhelmed. I doze off, imagining the many museums on the globe to visit to peer into the corpora of Indus script inscriptions, to see what messages our ancestors tried to convey.

Chapter 4 Sea-faring Sagan

'Our ancestors were boat-people. They were sea-faring merchants,' said Sagan with pride brimming in his half-closed eye-lids.

I nodded.

Sagan continued with a tinge of sorrow in his voice, 'Riverine waterways linking Adh Badri through Kunal, Banawali, Kalibangan, Dholavira, Nal Sarovar, Lothal have disappeared. The navigation link between Dholavira, Rann of Kutch and Baghdad, Tigris Euphrates rivers is still there. Navigating across the Persian Gulf, I should be able to carry carnelian stones and beads to Sumer.'

'Will Shu-ilishu be there to interpret you?' I asked, provocatively reminding him of the cylinder seal.

Sagan was not provoked. With a raised voice, he said,'Not to worry. We will carry the copper plates, seals and tablets which have the messages. We have the perforated beads. People of Elam will understand the metaphor of the swimming fish and the rim of the narrow-necked jar. Karmi will carry the alchemist's pot, the *kamaṇḍalu. Elo, elelo,* start the boatmans' song.' Sagan was clearly getting nostalgic, lapsing into rhyme and verse, caught up in a time-warp. The passage of time was suspended.

Was Sagan remembering the ligatured metaphor of goat and fish or *suhur mash* on the Sumer sacred basin? I was not sure, if I should ask Sagan about the two copper ox-hide ingots between the trees and birds carried on the boat on an Indus script tablet.

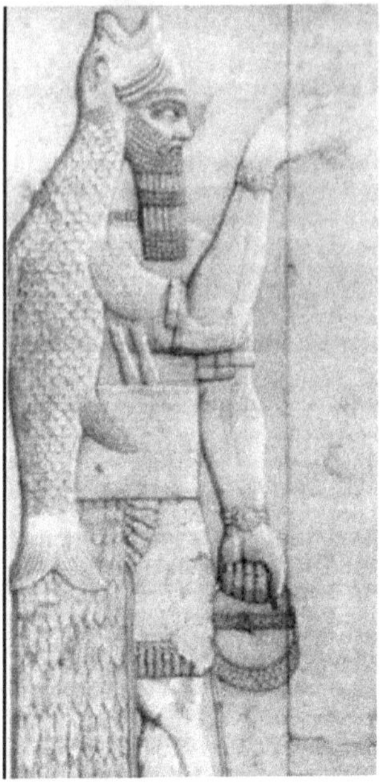

Suddenly, Sagan called Karmi Hatu, 'Tell this old man that we are all Sarasvati's children.' Was Sagan reminding me of the Brahm River which had existed before the Himalaya was formed by Varāha uprooting the earth in the Eurasian plate? If the Indian plate burst asunder the River Brahm, how come there is only a masculine river named Brahmaputra? Was Sarasvati Brāhmi the writing system for Vāk? I recollected the course of River Brahmaputra near Manas, Arunachal Pradesh, 14 kilometers wide and taking an acute U-turn, as if reversing course, trying to create another *sangam* 'confluence' with Ganga.

Sagan left me wondering why *śutudrī* flowing southwards from Siwaliks into River Sarasvati got deflected by a 90 degree turn at Ropar. Our ancestors of Ropar have left behind a tablet with inscriptions.

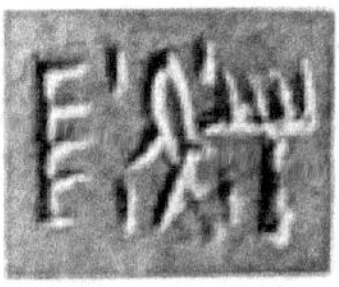

Ropar 1,Text 9021(One side of the tablet has two incised circles; the other side has three glyphs of Indus script).

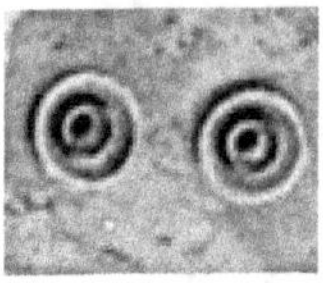

Were they dislocated by the type of earthquake which shook Bhuj on 26 January 2001, a quake caused by plate tectonics? Did the migratory turn by *śutudrī* leave Sarasvati high and dry? 'Sagan, are you, Karmi and me abandoned by *śutudrī* to deny us the sacred waters of Manasarovar glaciers?'

Why was our Mother angry with us? What went wrong that Sarasvati stopped flowing for us? Are the mysteries of Brahm unfathomable?

Chapter 5 Mother is merciful

'Our Mother will never desert us,' Sagan consoled me.

I accompanied Sagan to Gedra Road in Barmer District to take a dip in the sacred waters of Sarasvati flowing in a 40-feet wide, 12-feet deep canal originating from Harike reservoir formed from the dammed up waters of *śutudrī* with Bhakra-Nangal dam and of Vitastā.with Pong dam.

Madhav Pi was ecstatic. 'It is a magnificent spectacle to see the people of Jodhpur, Jaisalmer and Gedra Road quenching their thirst with the glacier waters from Manasarovar. Blessed are we, Sarasvati's children.' Madhav was a Secretary in the Ministry of Water Resources, Government of India, a recipient of the prestigious Stockholm Prize. Experts like him are role models for young scientists and technology students driven by an intense desire to serve poor people.

I remembered an incident that occurred as the search team for Sarasvati travelled in the month of May from Jodhpur to Nagaur. *En route*, all the containers of drinking water we carried had been emptied to quench our thirst in the sweltering 42-degree centigrade heat. We reached a village and as we approached a watering station, we saw a girl serving pilgrims with water from the pot in front of her. She served us too with a lot of joy, exclaiming, 'Ambā mā'. Guru asked that little girl, 'where do you get the pot of water from?' The girl responded in a clear, emphatic tone: 'I fetch this pot from Bhoj rāja's well which is only 10 kilometers from here.'

'Do you fetch the water every day?' I asked.

She said, 'yes,' and added, 'this is my life, I do not go to school, my mother has asked me to do this every day.'

Guru and I were left breathless. Bhoj rāja? He lived a thousand years ago. And, this girl gets the pot of water from a well dug by Bhoj rāja. What is all the development during the last 1000 years for? Could we not provide a well like Bhoj rāja's well in the girl's village? If we do that, the girl will go to school, once her mother is assured of tapped drinking water in the village.

'What is our prayer to Sarasvati?' Guru asked rhetorically, without expecting an answer. He added in a measured tone like the girl's tone, 'we have to make this girl go to school. That will be our prayer to Sarasvati.'

With that prayer, the convoy of vehicles moved on to visit the Jaina temple in Nagaur.

In that summer heat which could evaporate over 30% the waters of the Sarasvati canal, we could not even cry and shed tears as the girl waved to us, wishing us happy pilgrimage, 'Bye, bye. *śubh yātrā'.*

We realized that Devi Sarasvati is the divinity of education. That Mother should bless that girl and motivate her mother to enrol her in the village school.

Chapter 6 Song and dance in Rajasthan

Charan are singing bards of Rajasthan. They sing the song of 'Ambā Naī mā'.

Like Gritsamada, they call the river, Naī, Rajasthani form of Nadī.'

The annual mela on the dry river bed is filled with song and dance. Wearing colorful attire, ornamented with conch and terracotta or glass bangles from the wrists to the shoulders, wearing jingling anklets, the dancers sing the lullabies to put their children to sleep.

Burial ornaments made of shell beads and *turbinella pyrum* conch-shell bangle in a tomb at Mehergarh dated to circa 6500 BCE.

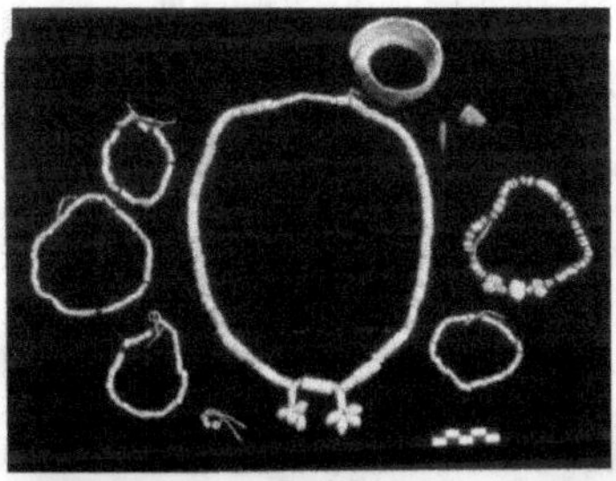

Mohenjodaro. One libation vessel made of conch shell (*turbinella pyrum*) is decorated with vermilion filled incised lines. A single spiraling design is carved around the apex and a double incised line frames the edge of the orifice. The vessel was also used to administer sacred water or medicine to children and patients.

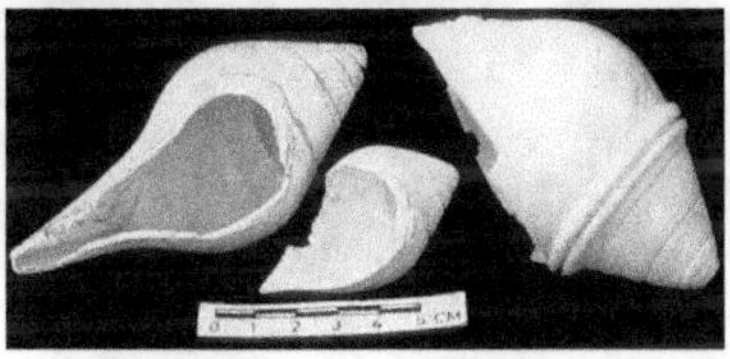

Guru reminded us of the pilgrimage places visited by Balarāma, the elder brother of Kṛṣṇa, narrating the verses from the *śalyaparva* of Mahābhārata, the Great Epic describing the journey from Somnath to *plakṣapraśravaṇa* in the Himalaya along the course of Sarasvati river. He took us to Pṛthudaka (Pehoa) near Kurukṣetra. This was the pilgrimage place where Balarāma offered oblations remembering his maternal ancestors. 'Gaya is famed for *pitṛśrāddham*, oblations to paternal ancestors. Pehoa is for *mātṛśrāddham*.' With such responsibilities entrusted to us, our ancestors have given us an abiding tradition. The reason is very simple. Our ancestors are our very identity. They are our *gestalt*.

I can understand why River Sarasvati was fondly called Mother, mā, Ambā.

In my search with Guru for Sarasvati, I tried to find an answer to the question: Why was she called Devi? Why was she, Mother genetrix, divine?

Was it because she spoke? Hence, she was called Vāk? Was she the cause of human capacity for speech communication?

Winds blow fiercely and create a dust storm. The dust rises upto 10,000 metres high and gets deposited hundreds of kilometers away. Was my Mother caught up in the dust storms of the rainless, summer months?

The earth she nourished has not also been kind to her. The earth rumbles again and again.

Sagan and I visited Bhuj after the devastation caused by the plate tectonic movement. The small brick houses had been reduced to rubble and families were huddled in front of the rubble surrounded by the salt marshes. Far away from the marshes, the waves of the sea ebbed and flowed into the Straits of Hormuz, often called the Persian Gulf.

Sagan wondered, 'That Shu-ilishu, seated like a child on the lap of the Sumerian merchant should have been a friend of our ancestors.'

Along the Gulf, many archaeologists have unearthed from many sites a number of seals and tablets which attest to the Meluhha artisans and traders at work.

Sagan continued his rambling account of what our ancestors did. 'I wonder what the boatmen carried on their onward journey to Sumer and what articles they brought back home. Surely, some of the articles were measured or weighed and accounted for on some records. Were they zoologists who were fond of animals, fascinated by the animals domesticated and wild? Have you seen the elephant or boar shown on some seals? Even as they sailed on their boats, did they know that Varāha was at work lifting up the earth and rendering streams into puddles expanding into lakes?'

'Maybe, they didn't pray enough to Sarasvati?' I hesitantly queried.

There was anger in Sagan's voice as he looked straight into my eyes. 'What a question to ask. She was the very being of fertility of the land. She made the land fertile with the waters and mineral pebbles. She was their life. She was their path. She was the light that lighted their path. She was the flow of their lives. She was the carrier of the wealth they accumulated. She was everything in their life mission, as the copper oxide ores they carried on the boats were unloaded into baskets carried on the heads of hundreds of worshippers of the Mother in the temple. The beads of carnelian and agate were stored and carried in pots, like the conical-bottom jars shown behind the Sumerian merchant on the Shu-ilishu seal.'

Sagan berthed the boat near a wharf in Dholavira where the glacial river joined the salty Indian ocean.

He opened the little jar of millet porridge and offered me my share. Sagan's mother was an expert in making millet porridge mixed with rock salt and pinch of fenugreek powder laced with fragrant coriander leaves. The delicious taste of the porridge made us remember Sagan's mother, leaving us wondering what work Karmi Hatu was doing, helping Sagan's mother.

As the clouds started thundering, Sagan and I took the oars, dipped them into the beating waves and let the boat float westward into the Gulf. A young girl on the shore waved us good-bye, shouting, 'May the Mother Divine be with you.'

Chapter 7 Migrating hamsa birds

As the boat tossed its way into the Gulf, a flock of hamsa flew above us, in a V-formation, as if answering and reinforcing the wishes of the girl on the shore wishing us *bon voyage*.

Sagan called it a good sign, a sacred augury, 'The hamsa are showing us the way. You know what? Hamsa are messengers from our ancestors. Hamsa fly long distances and even above the heights of the Himalayas in their annual migrations. I am a hamsa watcher. Hamsa are our path-finders and will tell us when we reach the shore to exchange greetings with the merchants of the Gulf eagerly awaiting our arrival.'

'Its amazing the way the hamsa birds fly in formation. So well-organized and determined they are. I wonder who taught them the path of their regular migration across the Himalayan heights.' I knew Sagan will be provoked to answer about our ancestors in the form of these birds, like the two additional forms of Mother and Divinity, assumed by River Sarasvati.

Sagan was in an expansive mood as he talked like the rishis of yore. 'Divine manifestations like the Universe, like the Brahman. You told me that Keshav and Mohan have trekked on the Himalayan glaciers and have written about the uprooting by Varāha. It is an abiding metaphor, this Varāha who lifts up Mother Universe and also carries her on his left shoulder. The right shoulder is reserved for carrying the form of Wealth Divinity, Lakṣmi. You know how Garuḍa carries Viṣṇu on the celestial skies. These hamsa birds remind us of Garuḍa, the way he extricated the elephant from the jaws of a crocodile. These hamsa float in the celestial oceans and they know how to reach their destinations in their annual pilgrimage. They remind us of our responsibility, our debt to perform these pilgrims' journeys. As the pilgrims' progress gets registered, there is a guy keeping a record of actions on the Universe. If Garuḍa is the *vāhana* of Viṣṇu,

Hamsa is the *vāhana* of Brahma. These Hamsa birds are on a universal journey of *ātman*, the Brahman.'

I couldn't unravel the mystery of the *Brahman*. How can it be *pūrṇa*, infinity or abundance and how can *ātman* also be *pūrṇa*, infinity. That are you, *tat tvam asi*. Such insights have made atomic scientists and geneticists wonder how a genome could carry a Universe of information, infinity within infinity. We are sailing on this boat for wealth, for abundance of our kith and kin. Sagan's mother makes exquisite millet porridge. The taste of the coriander leaves still lingers in the brain's memory and wafts in the air like the hamsa flying, flapping their strong wings in unison and in carefree abandon.

'*Parama hamsa*,' I said, 'supreme hamsa', remembering the Rishi Viśwāmitra who uttered the mantra: *Viśwāmitrasya rakṣati brahmedam bhāratam janam*, 'this song of Viśwāmitra protects the people of bhāratam.'

'Yes, the dharma of our ancestors, these hamsa protect us and children of this and future generations,' responded Sagan, trying to turn the boat right to avoid a jutting fishing float on the Gulf. The people of the Gulf were entrepreneurs. They could dive for pearls and conch shells to be brought ashore to be sawn into conches to blow the bugle of victory or to make a wake-up call. The sound of the conches soothe the boatmen and keep them awake till the journey's end.

The gaggle of geese are of the Anatidae family. In Irish, they are called *gē*, in Latin *anser*, in Czech *husa*, in Persian *ghāz*, in Finnish *hanhi*, Avestan *zāō*, in Russian *гусь*. When in flight, they are called a skein or a team. When flying close together, they are called a plump. They have been around for 10 million years since the Miocene age, according to the fossil record of North America. Miocene is a geological epoch extending from 23 to 5300 million years ago. Parama Hamsa are the *paramātman*.

Geese live in permanent pairs sustaining the monogamous dharma of marriage. Paired geese feed the goslings, the way Sarasvati feeds her children.

Do the hamsa teach us a lesson for being and becoming? They certainly are known for charting definite migratory paths over thousands of kilometers with a stunning precision that would put boat people to shame who navigate to America and end up in Australia, blaming the trade-winds for the loss of direction and destination.

I cannot count *pūrṇa*, even if I live infinite life-times. Life goes on as the boat gets tossed by the winds while Sagan and I rest the oars, allowing the winds to take us to our destination wharf.

Chapter 8 Louvre Museum and Looking for Shu-ilishu

Matching the search for Sarasvati is the search for someone from the descendants of Shu-ilishu.

Sagan was hopeful that he will find someone who, like Shu-ilishu speaks the languages of both Sumer and Vāk since he intuitively knew that the Meluhha merchant spoke the language of Vāk.

The curators of the Berlin and Louvre museums were most helpful. The Berlin curator showed us and explained to us the replica of the Sanchi stupa. It was a

commemoration, a remembrance of the ancestors whose ashes were kept in urns in the center of the dome carefully, meticulously engineered together with entrance arches with sculptures of elephants, lions, women clinging to creepers, worshippers meditating under the banyan tree at a nearby non-rusting dhvaja of Garuḍa as the vāhana of Viṣṇu. Sagan and I have often wondered how our ancestors produced the non-rusting iron pillar. The curator of Musée du Louvre showed us the goat-fish stone basin.

The basin was made of limestone. It perhaps dates from 1000 years ago. The ligatured goat-fish flank mollusks assembled together like a flagpost.

A similar structural formation of mollusks occur on theMathura Lion Capital. The word *hangi*in Kashmiri means a molluskc, read rebus *sangi*'a caravan of pilgrims'. Were the goat-fish on the Susa basin venerating the caravan of pilgrims? Were they using a Meluhha language metaphor to orthographically represent a formation of mollusks?

The curator explained that the basin is a symbol of the water cycle, Apsu, the body of the fresh water lying beneath the earth like Apsu denoted by *vāgāmbhṛṇī* Sarasvati .

It is the realm of the Divine. Who are we to fathom the mysteries of the realm?

The curator took us to another exhibit, the bronze of Sit-Shamshi which also

commemorated Apsu or Ea.

That bronze sculpture was breath-taking.

The bronze metaphor brought us to images of people at work or people at prayer. Maybe celebrants remembering their ancestors and their dharma?

Copper/bronze plate with vertical sides, 4.3 cm. height, 30.3 cm. dia. Mohenjodaro.

Were they the workers like Sagan, the legatees of a tradition, who would later create the iron pillar as Garuḍa dhvaja of Viṣṇu?

Heliodorus Garuḍa dhvaja of Viṣṇu at Vidisha, Besnagar dated to circa 120 BCE.

Of course, Sagan handled copper and zinc to make his brass vessels. His brass foundry had been known as the most ancient and famous foundry of Haryana.

This Harappa vessel contained a hoard of

copper weapons and tools. Ledged brass cooking vessel 16.5 cm height, 21 cm max. dia. with high neck and flaring rim, was made by hammering a sheet of copper alloy and raising the hollow base and rim separately. The two pieces were joined together with cold hammering at the ledge.

Many pilgrims visiting Adh Badri would pay a visit to Sagan's foundry to look at the trade mark pots he makes. These brass vessels should get a Trade Mark and a Jagadhri Geographical Indicator Mark the way the Mohenjodaro dancing girl of bronze makes her mark. It is a long process, this patenting and trade-marking process.

Like Guru who was confident that our team would find Sarasvati, Sagan was also brimming with optimism that he would learn from Shu-ilishu's descendant the languages of Sumerian and Vāk. How was he sure that Vāk was the language that the Meluhha merchant on Shu-ilishu cylinder seal spoke?

If hopes are dupes, said my teacher, fears are liars. Fear not. Awake. Move.

Chapter 9 Awake, move

Kaṭha upaniṣad was translated as 'The Secret of Death' by Edwin Arnold. Ralph Waldo Emerson also referred to it in his essay, 'Immortality'. It is the story of an encounter with Yama, of Nachiketa, son of Rishi Vājaśravasa. Yama teaches Nachiketa about true immortality. Kaṭha Rishi was a student of Vaiśampāyana.

Kaṭha means 'distress'. Upaniṣad means the 'mystery which underlies external system of phenomena'. Kaṭha upaniṣad is a novel, a narrative to awaken from distress. Material distress is ephemeral. Awaken to *Brahman*.

Ātman is the chariot's passenger. Body is the chariot. Buddhi is the charioteer. Mind is the reins. Five senses are the five horses drawing the chariot. Make everything still in Yoga.

Yama thunders:

uttiṣṭhata, jāgrata, prāpya varānnibodhata 'Arise, awake, and learn by approaching the exalted teachers.' That path is sharp like a razor's edge, impassable, so say the poets.

So it is that Somerset Maugham's epigraph reads, 'The sharp edge of a razor is difficult to pass over, thus the wise say the path to Salvation is hard.'

Sagan and I felt as though we were on a path to Salvation as our search for Shu-ilishu's descandants led us to the languages of the region. I ended up constructing a lexicon for over 25 ancient languages of *bhāratam,* and it took 20 years of my life. The lexicon is a start, but incomplete, because one life-time is not enough to attain immortality even as Sagan and I arise and are awake.

It is not mere coincidence that Plato also deploys the chariot allegory in Phaedrus dialogue to show the journey of the human *ātman*. Plato's chariot had only two winged horses. '...one of the horses is noble and of noble breed, but the other quite the opposite in breed and character. Therefore in our case the driving is necessarily difficult and troublesome,' notes Plato as he describes a 'great circuit' to follow the divinities in the path of enlightenment

Love is a divine madness,'...it traverses the whole heaven, appearing sometimes in one form and sometimes in another; now when it is perfect'.

J. de Morgan had excavated the bronze Sit-Shamshi masterpiece in 1904 from the Tell of the Acropolis, Susa Chogha Zambil close to a ziggurat and said to represent the ceremony of the rising sun. It is displayed in Room 10 Ground Floor, Display case 13 of the cute museum as cute as the Ropar museum.

One thing excited Sagan beyond compare. The bronze model was made by craftsmen of Elam who had acquired new metallurgical techniques. Sagan has no clue as to how his father and mother taught him the techniques of making brass pots which are in great demand from the residents of Adh Badri. Sagan also knew that Mohenjodaro yielded a bronze dancing girl, yes, the same girl also shown on a potsherd of Bhirrana, together with seals, on the banks of River Sarasvati discovered by archaeologist L.S. Rao.

Karmi Hatu also tends to haughtily put her right hand on her waist, just above the hip, striking a dance pose to annoy Sagan when he messes up the alloying of copper and zinc obtained from Khetri and Zawar, respectively.

Zinc smelting furnaces at Zawar, Rajasthan. A technique used to distil non-metallic zinc vapor using a retort. Zinc was added to copper to create brass alloy.

'Cross section through a zinc-smelting retort, 14–16th centuries, Zawar. A conical clay condenser tube was then securely luted to the open end of the retort and a stick was inserted to stop the charge from falling out when inverted and to create a central channel down which the zinc vapor could pass."

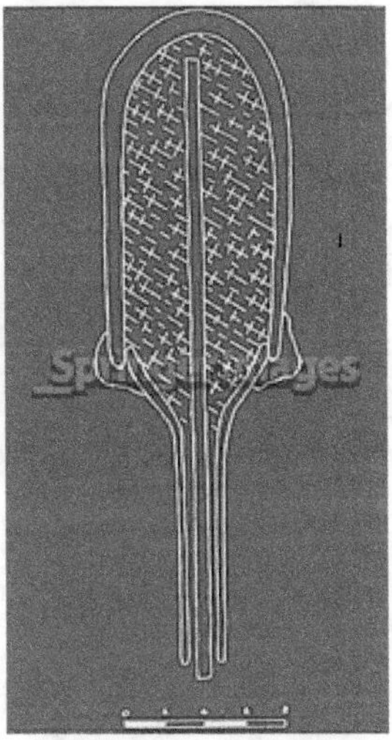

In the olden days, after the Sarasvati dried up, these minerals copper and zinc were brought by merchants driving donkey caravans. Nowadays, sometimes they arrive by train from Jodhpur to meet the inventory needs of Sagan's brass pot foundry industrial complex.

Sagan would exclaim when the shipment arrives: 'These are the pathways of accumulating gold. Brass is gold. I know the tricks of the trade, learnt from my ancestors.' Karmi Hatu helps him by carrying the *kamaṇḍalu* with the magic alchemical extract from herbs which transmutes copper into gold.

He knows how to attain immortality by doing his work.

L.S. Rao, archaeologist came close to seeing the dancing girl during Bhirrana excavations. He refers to the artist's rendering on the potsherd, 'Delineation is so true to the stance of the bronze sculpture including the dispensation of the girl's hands. It appears that the craftsman who drew the figure on the potsherd had seen the bronze girl of Mohenjodaro. She has tilter her head, legs are flexed. Her right hand rests on her waist, just above the hip. Her left hand is suspended by th side. Although nude, the bronze sculpture, 11 cm. high, is shown wearing a necklace, wristlets and armlets.'

I did not realize that an archaeologist has also to be an art critic to enjoy the legacy left for us to unravel. Rao continued to wax eloquent. 'The potsherd figure is stylized. Her torso resembles an hour-glass or like two triangles meeting at their apex. Upon the horizontal shoulder line, a partly damaged head was visible. Like the bronze girl, here too, the right hand is akimbo, left suspended by its side. Tender oblique strokes on the right upper arm are suggestive of the presence of armlets. The lower portion of the body is missing in the damaged sherd.'

Rao dug deeper until he reached the base level and found that Bhirrana settlement was continuously occupied from 7th millennium BCE.

Rao continued the artwork critique on the potsherd, 'Unlike the bronze girl, the potsherd girl was clothed. Clothing is indicated by horizontal hatchings on the chest and abdomen and vertical hatchings on the thighs.'

One fact is proved by geologist teams that Bhirrana, Banawali, Kalibangan and Kunal were ancient settlements of people on the ancient channel of *śutudrī* which was a tributary of River Sarasvati and which lies buried in the aolean sands brought in by the *āndhi* storms, year after year. The dust-storms create such a fog that flights get cancelled in the region due to zero visibility.

Sagan hugged Rao and told him just days before Yama of Nachiketa took Rao away 'You have seen the dancing girl. You are a lucky scholar. You have attained immortality, with a story to narrate about our ancestors of 7th millennium BCE.'

Chapter 10 Star gazers

Sagan respected star gazers. Many of them would come to his brass foundry to buy the utensils they needed for performing their daily puja and offerings of oblations to the manes. This is *samskāra*, which literally means 'putting together.'

The performer of puja forms turmeric cones, adorns the plate with offerings of betel leaves and flowers, adorns the forms of divinities, purifies and cleanses with water offering after every invocation, uses polished gems or finely ground sacred sāligrama stones to sanctify the puja. All these processes of making perfect constitute *samskāra*, a tribute to the discipline of the devotee offering his or her prayers. *Samskāra* is a sacred, sanctifying ceremony, one which purifies from the taint contracted in the womb to the consequent stages of life including the ceremony performed during cremation and thereafter in annual days of remembrance once the body becomes an ancestor. *Samskāra* is an impression of the mind as the body moves from being to becoming. So, it is a sacred celebration, performed with utmost discipline and utter dedication to *Brahman*.

Samskāra are performed strictly according to the calendar date and time consonant with the constellation map of the sky. Time is sacred, so is space.

Vaiśampāyana the narrator of the Mahābhārata to Janamejaya, was a star gazer. He was also a student of Vyāsa.

A historian par excellence, Vaiśampāyana records the precise time of events – precise to the minute subatomic time of the celestial clock, using the sky map as the 'calendar-clock' as the events unfolded on the Sarasvati river basin.

He records the date and time when Balarāma started on his pilgrimage along River Sarasvati and the date and time when he returned to Dwāraka.

'Balarāma sets off on pilgrimage on Sarasvati on Puṣya day Nov. 1, 3067 BCE .Balarāma returns from pilgrimage on Śravaṇa day Dec. 12, 3067 BCE,' said Narahari showing us the sky maps of the dates as seen on Planetaria software.

During this travel, Balarāma sees brothers quarrelling with one another, leading to war which started on Nov. 22, 3067 BCE.

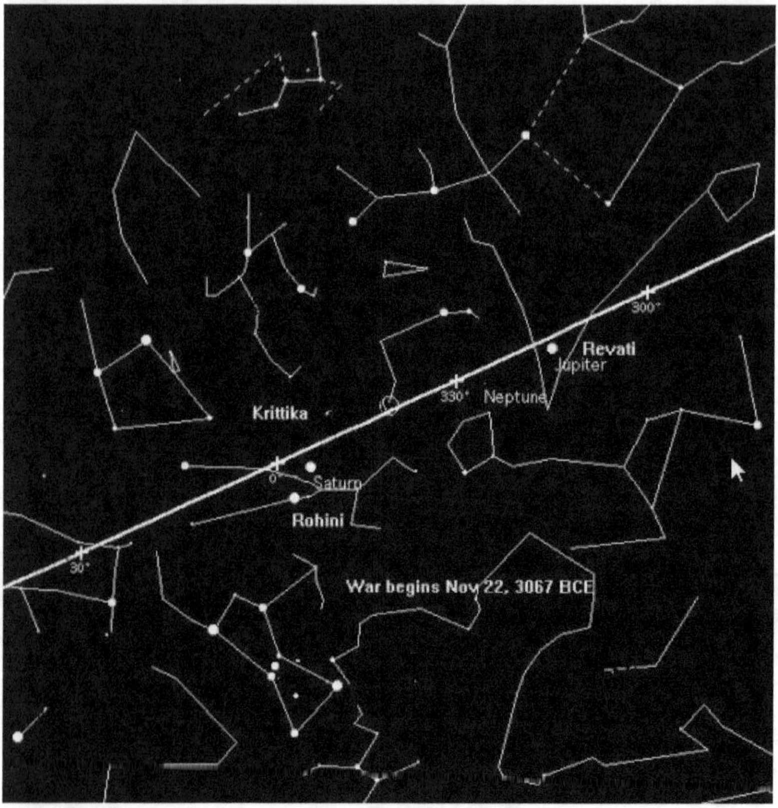

The narrator also records that Balarāma witnessed the *gadāyuddha* (fight with a mace) between Duryodhana and Bhima and refused to take sides in the ongoing war between brothers. He returns to his responsibility as an agriculturist.

Sagan realized that he has set in motion, thanks to Guru, and was part of, a quest to zero-in on the locus of River Sarasvati and the date when she started deserting our ancestors.

Chapter 11 Doodles? Corpora of focused glyphs?

Experts trace the writing to circa 3300 BCE on the banks of River Ravi in Harappa, that is about the same time, cuneiform writing system was evolving in Sumer to keep accounts. This date makes it a writing system earlier than the Egyptian hieroglyphs on Narmer Palette

Seal, Mohenjodaro. The glyphs are: a

pair of bulls, a crocodile, a boar or rhinoceros, a monkey, an elephant, an antelope, fish.

Were they zoo-keepers or zoologists with specialization in aquatic species? Did the glyphs have 'meaning'?

Sagan was not interested in my attempts to search for 'meanings'. For Sagan, these attempts are *vyartha,* (useless, vain, fruitless, unprofitable' I was surprised that Sagan should be looking for 'profit', a process out of character with his world-view of seva, self-less service. The compound *vyartha* includes the lexeme *artha* which means 'object, purpose, desire, wealth'. Sagan was worldly-wise and the owner of a brass foundry in Jagadhri which was becoming a world-famous tourist attraction, for metallurgists trying to unravel the techniques of smiths as they evolved over millennia.

Philosophers will ask *kimartham*, for what purpose, why'.

I don't know. Why do people climb mountains?

Because they are there. A testimony to the vagaries of the earth in perpetual motion, with Varāha operating in Bharatam jutting into and lifting up the Eurasian plate.

It is a primordial, cosmic dance, like Śiva's *tāṇḍavam*. This dance pose has fascinated nuclear scientists. Śiva-Naṭarāja's cosmic dance is kept like an open-air temple at CERN, European Center for Research in Particle Physics in Genova. There are indications that our ancestors of Bhirrana knew of this exquisite dance step, which is as exciting as the bronze dancing-girl's or potsherd dancing-girl's provocative pose.

Sagan's encounter with Viśwakarma comes to mind. He asked Viśwakarma of Swamimalai in Tamil Nadu, 'How come you make Nataraja bronzes using the same *cire perdue* technique deployed by our ancestors who made the bronze dancing girl?'

The response was instructive. Viśwakarma said, 'I know why you ask this question. Our ancestors taught us this lost-wax technique for making bronze metaphors of reality. Song and dance are part of our lives, Sagan. Just look at the folks in Rajasthan. The Charans and the women carrying pots of water from Sarasvati sarovar sing and dance to the cosmic rhythm, the *ṛta*.'

I knew that *ṛta* was a pious action or custom, a divine law, a divine truth. It was a form of *dharma* that had become the meaning of our lives, the meaning of lives of our ancestors.

I have transgressed far from the corpora. I am avoiding the process of understanding the messages our ancestors have left for us prescribing righteous rules of living. *Ṛta* is also truth, the very *raison d'etre* of life.

Why did CERN choose the metaphor of the cosmic dance? To remind scientists of the cosmic dance of subatomic particles which were observed, analyzed by CERN physicists? It is good to see a scientist like Fritjof Capra write, in 1972,.an article titled 'The Dance of Shiva: the Hindu view of matter in the light of modern physics' in *Main Currents in Modern Thought*. Capra repeated this metaphor in *The Tao of Physics.*

I have digressed indeed from corpora to Physics.

A plaque accompanies the statue at CERN offering an explanation; since it is by scientists, I will reproduce it verbatim and in full:

> Ananda K. Coomaraswamy, seeing beyond the unsurpassed rhythm, beauty, power and grace of the Nataraja, once wrote of it "It is the clearest image of the activity of God which any art or religion can boast of."
>
> More recently, Fritjof Capra explained that "Modern physics has shown that the rhythm of creation and destruction is not only manifest in the turn of the seasons and in the birth and death of all living creatures, but is also the very essence of inorganic matter," and that "For the modern physicists, then, Shiva's dance is the dance of subatomic matter."
>
> It is indeed as Capra concluded: "Hundreds of years ago, Indian artists created visual images of dancing Shivas in a beautiful series of bronzes. In our time, physicists have used the most advanced technology to

> portray the patterns of the cosmic dance. The metaphor of the cosmic dance thus unifies ancient mythology, religious art and modern physics."

Now, I understand why this excurcus is important to understand the 'meaning' of glyphs in the corpora. The Corpora are a record of advances in technology for accumulating *artha*, wealth and to sustain the wealth of nations which is not only a life-process but an end in itself to provide *abhyudayam* to society.

Sagan sat in silent meditation.

The Susa ritual basin was part of the process.

Viśwakarma's ancestors who dealt with metal tools and vessels, like Sagan, also dealt with writing about them using glyphs like 'fish' glyph on the Susa pot.

Sagan did not respond. He was fast asleep, maybe, in *yoga nidrā*, like the sleep of Viṣṇu at the end of a Yuga. Patañjali's work on yoga is also called *yoga nidrā śāstram* 'science of yoga contemplation.'

Chapter 12 Dynamic Himalayan millennia

Keshav reminisces, lapsing into poetic imagery, after his trek in the Himalayas,

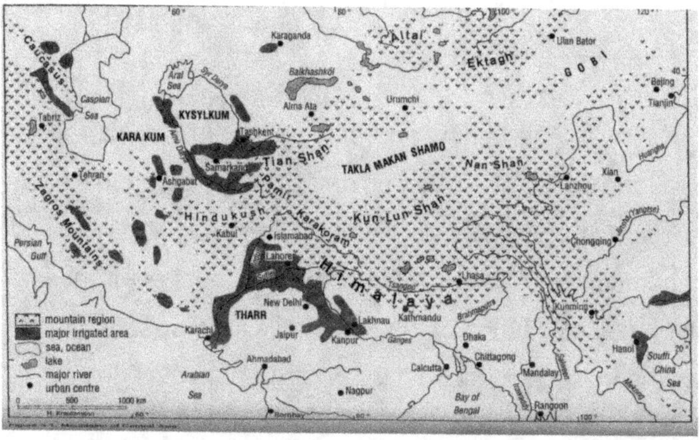

'Very young in age, the rugged Himalaya continues to be seized repeatedly with spells of tectonic restlessness or crustal disturbances...The giant body of the mountain quivers in some segments or twitches spasmodically and breaks up violently in other places. These are manifestations of the tectonic turmoils of growing, for the Himalaya is still growing. Consequently, its framework of structure is recurrently deformed and the landscape reshaped time and again. It is the titanic force of compression resulting from the coming together and eventual collision of the continents of India and Asia that transformed the once enormous pile of sediments on the northern margin of the Indian shield into the Himalaya of immense splendor and magnificence.'

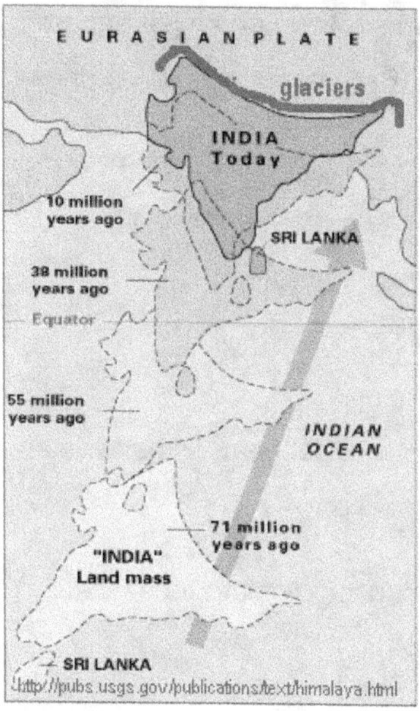

Himalayas extend from Teheran in Iran to Hanoi in Vietnam.

Himalaya is a 5200 km. long and 300 to 400 km. wide mountain chain, which abruptly rises above the vast expanse of the Indo-Gangetic plains, virtually isolating India from the rest of Eurasia. 1400 cubic kilometers of snow and ice spread over about 33,200 square kilometer area above the 4300 to 5800 m snowline. There are over 15,000 glaciers here. Many of these, on the Indian side, have been inventoried by glaciologist Mohan for World Glacial Inventory based in Zurich, Switzerland. These glaciers melt and contribute over 50 percent of the water flowing in the ten main Himalayan rivers.

The zone of collision of India with Asia is now occupied by Rivers Sindhu and Tsangpo-Brahmaputra and the drainages of Sutlej, and Karnali. About 65 million years ago, India with its island of volcanoes slammed against mainland Asia and completely welded itself to mainland Asia by about 55 million years ago. The basin formed as a result of the subsidence of the foreland is filled up with riverine sediments and constitute the Indo-Gangetic Plains. 'Four great rivers originate from the Kailas-Mansarovar tract in southwestern Tibet. The Sindhu flows northwestward, the Sutlej takes a southwesterly course, the Karnali (Ghaghara in the plains) descends southwards and the Tsangpo (Brahmaputra in India) goes east,' said Keshav.

Aravalli range held structural control over the drainage pattern providing the water-divide for east-flowing and west-flowing drainage rivers.

Violent crustal movements cause earthquakes.

- Indian plate is dynamic, it is still moving at 6 cm. per year; Himalayas are rising 1 cm. per year
- Result: formation of glaciers, earthquakes caused by plate tectonics
- 6000km. Journey of Bharata in 40-50 m. years
- Majority of the Earth's glaciers are found in the American Cordillera, Alps, and Himalaya. Each of these are areas of geologically recent (less

than 100 million years) mountain building associated with Plate Tectonics

Mountains cause disturbances in airflow, altering global circulation patterns.

Siwalik ranges about 250 to 800 m high are mere sediments deposited by ancient Himalayan rivers in the last 16 to 1 ½ million years.

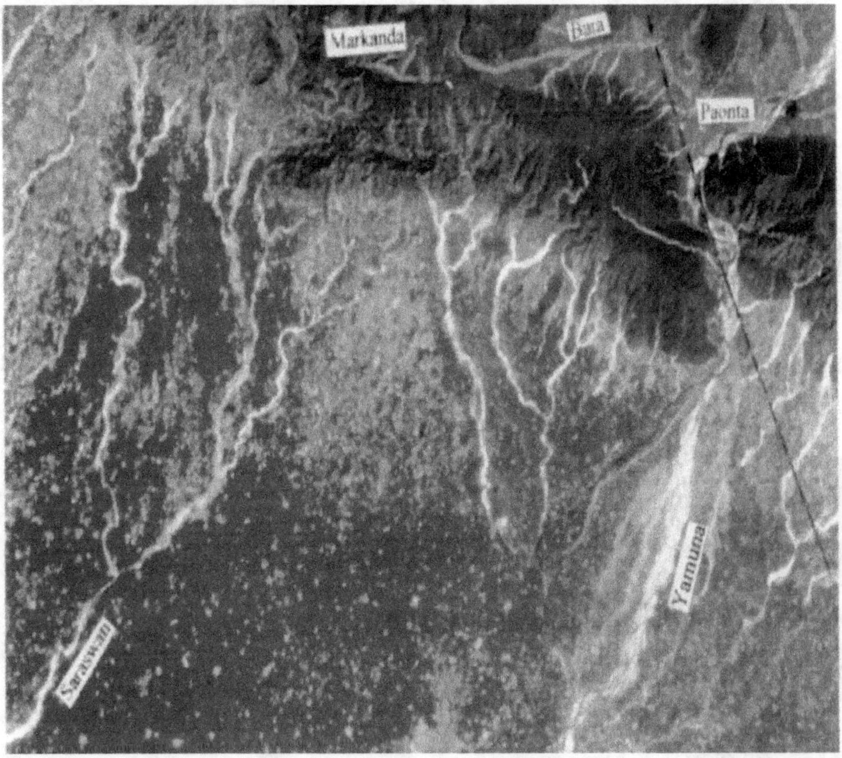

Satellite image which shows the pathsof Rivers Markanda, Sarasvati and Yamuna.

Siwalik hills were left-laterally displaced. NNW-SSE-trending tear fault is still active. The earlier west-flowing rivers were swung southwards, following the path of the fault which runs parallel to the Aravalli ranges which constitute the water-divide. Yamuna flows eastwards, Sutlej flows westwards.. Both drainages are along very gentle slopes. On the banks of River Yamuna, Agra's altitude is only

169 meters above sea level. Chandigarh's altitude is only 325 meters above sea level.

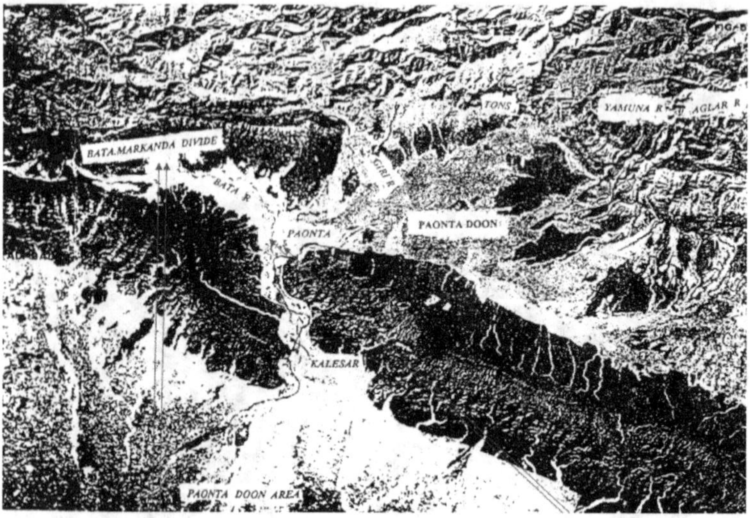

Bata-Markanda divide

Reborn Sarasvati.Mohangarh.40 ft.wide, 12 ft. deep (2007).

No wonder, the poet Kālidāsa described the Himalaya as devatātmā, divinity. In the Indian tradition, Śiva sits in penance on the summit of Kailas Mountain above the Manasarovar glacier, with River Ganga flowing from the locks of his hair. This is an ancient metaphor as exquisite as the cosmic dance metaphor.

One of three *śivalinga* found in situ, at Harappa, by Archaeologist Vats . The shape is like the summit of Mt. Kailas, Himalayas.

The traditional narrative told to me by my mother is that Śiva-Naṭarāja's cosmic dance finds another form, *rūpam* here – as a water-giver. The same way that Divinity Sarasvati assumes the *rūpam* of a River. Śiva is venerated in all temples by *abhiṣekam* performed in perpetuity, by allowing the water drops to drip from a water-pot placed above the Śivalinga. Śiva of Manasarovar and Sarasvati of Pehoa are both water divinities who have made it a sacred duty of millions of pilgrims to take a sacred dip in the waters seeking the discharge of *ṛṇam*, the debt of their lives.

The lost river Sarasvati is reborn with the waters of *śutudrī* (Sutlej) flowing through the 40 ft. wide 12 ft. deep channel from Harike reservoir created by the Bhakra-Nangal dam on River Sutlej and Pong dam on River Beas. It now traverses over 1000 kilometers from Harike to Gedra Road, Barmer, Rajasthan, just 150 kilometers to go to reach Gujarat.

Chapter 13 Muztagh Ata and Soma

This chapter should rightly be titled, Muztagh Ata, Tocharian, Silk Road, Sarasvati and Soma. Muztagh Ata (24,386 ft.) on the border of Tajikistan and China's Xinjiang, beyond the northeast frontier of Afghanistan, is close to the sources of Oxus and Yarkand-Tarim rivers.

All Tocharian language documents have been discovered along the Silk Road.

I will explain the importance of Tocharian in the search for Sarasvati closely associated with Vedic language.

Remember G.K. Chesterton's Father Brown's detective stories? One story is about a postman. I am recalling this narrative because Sagan's search for Sarasvati succeeds with surprising detective leads from unsuspected sources on the Silk Road, on the northern stretch of the Himalayas.

Let me quote extensively from tho 'Invisible Man' in 'The Innocence of Father Brown.'

> He took three quick strides forward, and put his hand on the shoulder of an ordinary passing postman who had bustled by them unnoticed under the shade of the trees.
>
> 'Nobody ever notices postmen somehow,' he said thoughtfully; 'yet they have passions like other men, and even carry large bags where a small corpse can be stowed quite easily.'

Detective Father Brown in his innocence had found the clue. The postman carried the corpse out of the house and was the prime suspect for the crime.

Almost all researchers agree that Rigveda is an ancient human document, a song *par excellence*, rendered with fidelity over millennia. Many also agree that the entire narrative of the song is *in nuce* (in a nutshell) in the precisely described purchase and processing of Soma, as a commodity. Almost all agree that Rigveda was first chanted on the banks of River Sarasvati. There are over 70 ṛks which extol the divinity of Sarasvati and the flow of Sarasvati as river from the mountains. So, it is on the banks of Sarasvati river that soma yajña was first performed. One narrative says that Soma was purchased from the sellers coming from Mount Mujāvata.

The reference in Rigveda reads: RV 10.34.1 *somasyeva maujavatasya bhakṣo vibhīdako jāgṛvir mahyam acchān*, 'an alerting eatable *vibhīdaka* and soma libation of Mount Mujāvata delight me.' *Vibhīdaka* is the berry of *Terminalia bellerica* tree, the berry is used as a die. No wonder the poet gets delighted playing dice ! Soma libation also delights him because it yields wealth.

The legitimate search for Mount Mujāvata leads us to Muztagh Ata peak of the Himalayas because Muztagh Ata, linguists say, is a cognate phonetic form, concordant with Mujāvata.

Assuming Muztagh Ata is the same as Mujāvata, one route is to travel along the Silk Road to get there.

But, the clue to identify Soma came, not from Muztagh Ata but from another World Sanskrit Conference held recently where a Professor George Pi presented a paper on the link between Tocharian language and Rigveda. Like me working on the Indian lexicon, George Pi has contributed to the compilation of a Tocharian lexicon. In that paper, he made the announcement that *amśu* of Rigveda is cognate with *ancu* of Tocharian.

The two words *amśu* and *ancu* have existed for millennia and as Father Brown said, 'Nobody ever notices postmen somehow.'

So, Sagan and I can say, 'Nobody ever notices *amśu* somehow'.

Many researchers have attempted the identification of Soma, but not many realized that *amśu* is used as a synonym of Soma in the ancient text, Rigveda itself.

So far, some researchers have assumed *amśu* to be a stalk of a leafless plant since there is no description of Soma leaves, though there are hints that processing of Soma could involve some herbals. Actually अंशु *amśu* has many meanings in Vedic *chandas* which has lexical cognates with Indo-European languages.

m. Pointed, Fibrous, abounding in filaments (especially of the सोम plant) अंशुती Name of a plant *Desmodium Gangeticum*

a kind of सोम libation

end of a thread , a minute particle; A cloth, garment in general Latin

A ray, beam of light अंशुमान् sun

अंश्य *a.* [अंश्-कर्मणि यत्] Divisible.

Name of a ऋषि RV. viii , 5 , 26; of an ancient Vedic teacher , son of a धनंजय; of a mountain

Some of the meanings out of this list have led some researchers to focus on identifying Soma as a herbal, offering many alternatives ranging from mushrooms to aphrodisiacs because of the excitement reported by some engaged in Soma processing.

George Pi's revelation of *ancu* as the linguistic equivalent of *amśu* provides a new detective lead. *Ancu* in Tocharian referred to a metallic mineral, NOT a plant. In ancient India, Tocharians were known as Tuṣāra, a word which occurs as name of a people in many Indian ancient texts. The word also means 'ice, snow' clearly pointing to their habitat, Mujāvata or Muztagh Ata as a snowy Himalayan mountain.

Ancu amśu as a metallic mineral ! Sagan was ecstatic, given his metallurgical skills. He exclaimed, 'if Soma was *ancu amśu* we have found the Tocharian merchants from the mountains from the Soma sellers coming from Mount Mujāvata. If Mujāvata was Muztagh Ata, we have found the source of metallic mineral Soma. It should be in the region neighboring Muztagh Ata.' Sagan knew the importance of Soma for his ancestors, Soma meant wealth, electrum.

George Pi's linguistic excursus in semantics and etymology provided some details of *ancu*. He had noted insightfully that many translations of nouns of Vedic language had been loaded with etymological prejudices, 'based on purported connections with verbal roots'. Maybe, Soma as *ancu amśu* had connections with Muztagh Ata as Mujāvata, the supply source of Soma, where Tocharian was spoken.

An excursus on whether Tocharian was an Indo-European language and hence with close connections to Vedic language need not detain us here.

Sagan knew that in the *magnum opus Science and Civilisation in China,* British biochemist and sinologist Joseph Needham had seen *asem, asemon* (Egyptian) meaing 'electrum' as cognates of soma. In Santali, a Munda language, *samanom* meant 'gold'. In Gypsy language, *somnakay* meant 'gold'. In Avestan, *haoma* (*hom*) meant 'soma'.

The annotations made in Tocharian thesaurus are:

> Another linguist Lubotsky notes that *ancu means 'soma plant'. This assumed word is said to be the source of Vedic language *amśu* which means 'soma plant'.

Cognates are Latin and Avestan *asu-* 'haoma plant'. One Vedic song reads: *amśur- amśus te deva somāpyāyatām indrāyaikadhanavide* 'let your *amśu* after *amśu* shine strong, O Soma – for Indra the winner of one part of the treasure'. Now that we know the synonym *ancu* means 'metal, iron', the translation of the song should read: 'let your metal after metal shine strong, O Soma – for Indra the winner of one part of the treasure.'

Derived from *añcu* 'iron' (Tocharian B *eñcuwo*, adj. *encuwanne* 'made of iron'). Note that Indo-European did not have a common word for 'iron'.

añcwāṣi adj. 'iron-; Nom.Sg.Masc.

Obl. Sg. Masc. *añcwāṣim*

Obl. Sg. Fem. *añcwāṣṣām*

Nom. Pl. Masc. *añcwāṣiñi*

Nom. Pl. Fem. *añcwāṣṣāñ*

Obl. Pl. Fem. *añcwāṣṣās*

Fish hieroglyphs of metalwork

Proto-Ugric **waS* 'metal, iron'; Proto-Baltic **waSke* 'copper, brass' and Old Prussian ausis, Tocharian B *yasa*,'gold', Tocharian A *was* 'gold' were possible ancient words dealing with metallic minerals, just as *aya, ayas* in ancient languages meant 'copper, bronze' – a word which could be denoted by the hieroglyph 'fish' like the one shown on Susa pot with metal tools and weapons.

This was the Susa pot with the 'fish' glyph found by Archaeologist Maurizio.

Sagan as an expert brass worker with an ancient brass foundry realized that he was getting close to understanding the importance of Soma in the entire Vedic corpora.

"Eureka!" he exclaimed and continued, "*añcwāṣi* of Tocharian is clearly a reduplication of *ancu* 'metal' + *waṣ* 'gold' (Tocharian A, Proto-Ugric). Note that Tocharian *yasa* 'gold' is cognate with Vedic *ayas* 'metal, bronze'; Tamil *ayil* 'iron'; Malayalam *ayir, ayiram* 'any metallic ore'. Many Indian languages had cognate words: *ayo* 'iron' of Pali, *aya* 'iron' of Prakrit, So Tocharian *ancu* is cognate with Vedic language *amśu* which should have meant 'gold'. Our ancestors performing soma yajña were processing a gold mineral called *ancu, amśu.* Now we can understand why the Susa pot had the 'fish' glyph to denote the contents of the pot which were exclusively metallic tools and weapons. The 'fish' glyph was *aya,* 'fish' in Munda, a Mleccha-Meluhha language of our ancestors."

This was a terracotta pot, unlike the brass pot which also contained metal tools and vessels.

"You are like Father Brown, Sagan. You have detected something extraordinary. You have not only found Sarasvati but also have provided a clue to the decipherment of Indus script corpora."

For the first time, in my decades of acquaintance with Sagan, I found that Sagan was blushing. He is a remarkably humble person and would not make vainglorious claims and make pontifical pronouncements.

It was indeed the first time that I had heard him utter the exclamation: "Eureka!"

'Oh, no. We have long way to go unraveling the messages left for us by our ancestors. One thing is clear. They were very literate people and artisans eager to experiment with new non-metallic minerals like zinc to polish brass to attain the glittering gold status.'

'Isn't it amazing that in one Sanskrit conference I report the finding of the channels of Sarasvati River. And, now, in another Sanskrit conference, George Pi reports the findings of the meaning of the Vedic language word *amśu.*'

Sagain replied, "You are right about Father Brown. Nobody notices a postman carrying a large bag which contained the corpse. But, it is the responsibility of those participating in Sanskrit conferences to help us find Sarasvati. She is the very *raison d'etre*, the reason for our being."

Let me repeat what Chesterton had said: 'The postman, instead of turning naturally, had ducked and tumbled against the garden fence.'

Hundreds of researchers have been at work trying to understand 1. Soma which is *in nuce* (in a nutshell) the message of the Vedas and 2. Indus script corpora with thousands of inscriptions.

Like the postman, we have ducked and tumbled.

Similarly, Tocharian *ancu* and Vedic language *amśu* could potentially refer to 'metal, iron'. George Pi's Tocharian lexicon work confirms this. *Ancu* meant 'iron'. Hence, Vedic language *amśu* might have meant 'electrum, gold'.

It is always a pilgrimage to set foot on the snows near glaciers of the Himalayas.

Sagan continued on his annual pilgrimage treks on the Himalayas. Normally when he goes such treks on the higher reaches of the Himalayas, he leaves the chores of brass foundry management to Karmi Hatu.

One such annual pilgrimage trek took him to Kyrgyzstan and Mount Muztagh Ata.

At the middle of the night, Sagan suddenly woke up startled by the cackling *Anser indicus* couple of geese. He knew they were a couple because he had read that a pair of geese may mate up for life, upto about 20 years. The female *Anser indicus* has a voice different from that of the male. The couple were leading their family of goslings on a parade. The goslings were in a line with the father *Anser* in the front and the mother *Anser* at the back. When flying, they make a V-shaped formation.

Sagan also knew that cackling *Anser* are found sometimes in eastern Siberia, throughout Japan and sometimes in eastern China. He was surprised to find the *Anser* parade at the foothills of Mount Muztagh Ata.

A dispute is raging among ornithologists in the *Journal of Ornithology*, if *Branta hutchinsii minima* or small cackling geese are a subspecies of *Anser Indicus*, though the former species are generally found in North America.

Anser indicus father, mother and family of goslings.

Characteristic feeding habits of *Anser* is that they feed mainly on plant material. Even while on water, they search out for aquatic plants, submerging their necks to reach out to the bottom of the lakes. They also eat crustaceans and mollusks. While swimming on water surface, they lift up their necks majestically and tip forward their necks like dabbling ducks.

Sagan was fascinated by the characteristic cackling of the geese and goslings in the parade.

Chapter 14 Sagan's pilgrimage to Muztagh Ata

Just as Mount Kailas overlooks the young Thar Desert of Rajasthan in India, Muztagh Ata overlooks China's vast desert of Takla Makan in Xinjiang.

Most of Xinjiang is of recent geological origin formed by the *Varāha*-type uplift of the Eurasian plate as the Indian plate thrust into it and kept moving northwards. Like Sarasvati River basin, Xinjiang is a major earthquake zone because of the plate tectonics.

Islamabad, Pakistan and Kashgar are linked by the Karakoram Highway over the Khunjerab Pass.

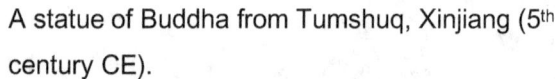

A statue of Buddha from Tumshuq, Xinjiang (5th century CE).

Any search for the people of Mujāvata who sold soma may have to include Uighur, Han, Kazakh, Tajik, Hui, Kyrgyz and Mongol who live in Xinjiang-Uighur Autonomous Regions of China, are sometimes referred to as Chinese Turkestan. This is also the region influenced by Tocharians and Kushans.

We do not know if the Yuezi people who supplied jade from Tarim Basin in ancient times were also the people who traded in *ancu amśu*, 'metal gold or perhaps, electrum.'

Connected to the Pamirs, Muztagh Ata (Uighur: مۇز تاغ ئاتا, literally means, "ice-mountain-father" and constitutes the northern edge of Tibetan Plateau.

Sagan and I decided that for our expedition, we will not choose the route taken by our ancestors trekking from Gandhara. We also avoided the bus route from Gilgit, Pakistan to Kashgar/Muztagh Ata which was a journey of 700 km. over 14 hours passing through the Khunjerab Pass. We chose the direct flight from London to Bishkek, Kyrgyzstan.

In Kyrgyzstan, after attaining independence due to the break-up of the Soviet Union, ruble was replaced by som as the currency. The word *som* means 'pure (gold)' in Kazakh, Kyrgyz, Uighur and Uzbek.

From Bishkek we travelled by a bus to Tash Rabat which is a historic caravanserai in Kyrgyzstan. After spending the night there in a yurt, another bus took us along Fergana Range and Torugart Pass. A third bus was a ride with a Chinese which took the bus on a descent into Kashgar, Xinjiang located on the Silk Route. The onward journey from Kashgar passed Mount Kongur and we spent the night at a yurt on the banks of Lake Karakol which was to the left of Muztagh Ata.

I continued to stay in the yurt, as Sagan started his trek from nearby Subashi to the base camp, located at a height of 4,450m, a trek of 4 hours. It took him and the trekking team which accompanied him 18 days to climb Muztagh Ata.

Saga returned to the yurt on the banks of Lake Karakol exhausted and still panting after successfully reaching the summit.

Together we rode the bus back to Kashgar, drove through the Torugart Pass to reach Tash Rabat en route to Bishkek. From Bishkek, we flew back to London.

Glaciated summit of Muztagh Ata and Karakol Lake

The pilgrimage was exhilarating for me because I had spent over 19 days at the Karakul Lake just watching the trekkers and caravans of camels on the nearby Karakoram Highway passes and continued to be overwhelmed by the awesome presence of Muztagh Ata, so far yet so near. I spent my days reading about explorer and cartographer, Sven Hedin's failed summit climb attempt on the back of a yak in 1894, browsing through his *Central Asia Atlas* and about expeditions along the Silk Road.

Here is a breathtaking satellite image composite of the Himalayan range.

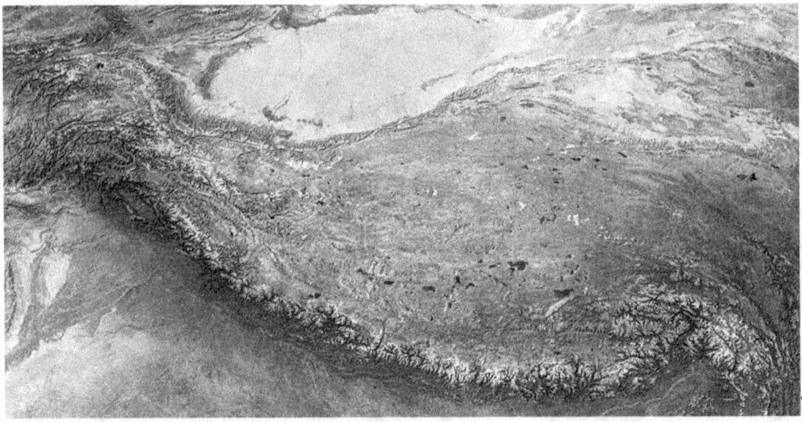

The Tibetan Plateau is near the center. Takla Makan desert is visible as the lighter area near the top.

I did not have the courage to make the 18-day climb to reach the summit but complimented Sagan for his successful climb to the summit at 7546 m.

I have called this a pilgrimage because any journey to any part of the Himalayan range is a pilgrimage to the peaks surrounding Mount Kailas where Śiva sits in penance on the summit, blessing the glaciers of Manasarovar on the foothills of Kailas.

To answer those who wonder why I have such a cryptic account of the pilgrimage undertaken with Sagan without explaining the inquiries we made about the supply centers for *ancu amśu*. Since this is a detective story, I will stay with this narrative, without elaborating on the gold belts of Dzungar (lit. left hand) in northern Xinjiang or Kyrgyzstan which could have provided the raw material for the soma sellers of Mujāvata of Vedic times.

For now, I will just leave this chapter with one tantalizing clue. The Greek and Roman name for Xinjiang was Seres. In a remarkable account of the Orient, Henry Yule notes in *Cathey and the way thither*:

> "The region of the Seres is a vast and populous country…The people are civilised men, of mild, just, and frugal temper, eschewing collisions with their neighbours, and even shy of close intercourse, but not averse to dispose of their own products, of which raw silk is the staple, but which include also silk stuffs, furs, and iron of remarkable quality."

Sagan has established some contacts with metal-workers of the region and got confirmation that *ancu amśu* indeed meant *som*, the name of the currency now used in Kyrgyzstan. Ethical reporting also dictates that I should mention the problems Sagan and I encountered after the Chinese armed guards detained us for questioning. The good news is that we were cleared of the initial charge of being spies from Switzerland banks after Sagan showed them a sample of the brass pot he had brought to be shown to metallurgists living on the foothills of Muztagh Ata and other Pamir range mountains and after I swore an affidavit that we were neither ornithologists looking for the habitat of *Anser indicus*, nor botanists or zoologists interested in collecting either samples of North Himalayan herbals or DNA samples from animals of the region. When we showed them the findings of George Pi, they showed no interest whatsoever. They looked at Sven Hedin's *Central Asia Atlas* which I was holding and carefully went through the pages to make sure that we had not annotated the printed maps. I should add that the guards were courteous and even offered us cups of hot Chinese herbal tea. They did not search our baggage but just looked at the currencies we carried, including some new notes of *som* from Kyrgyzstan and an Indonesian Rupiah.20000 currency note I had kept in my book as a page marker, because it contained the image of Tantra Vinayaka considered a Divine blessing for School Children. The currency note showed Vinayaka on the obverse and a classroom

on the reverse. I did not tell the guards that Sagan and I were promoting the formation of Indian Ocean Community like the European Community. Ki Hajar Dewantara shown on the currency note was the 1st Minister of National Education of the Republic of Indonesia.

Sarasvati is venerated in India as a metaphor Divinity of Education. On some traditional paintigs, a hamsa is shown next to her, sometimes a peacock.

Chapter 15 Sagan's sparks from the anvil and Shu-ilishu's language skills

I raised a series of questions and waited for Sagan's answers.

'What was Karmi Hatu carrying in the alchemical pot as she accompanied the Meluhha merchant interpreted by Shu-ilishu?'

'Did it contain the *amṛtam* elixir which could transmute Sagan's trade-mark Jagadhri brass into gold?'

'Were the sparks which came out of the brass plate which he beat to shape as a pot, lost gold particles?'

'Am I that spark?'

Sagan just smiled and read out the line from Kṛṣṇa's song divine: '*nimittamātram.bhava savyasācin*, yes, you are an instrument, a spark from Kṛṣṇa's anvil. Yes, Kṛṣṇa, like Newton, was an alchemist, he could transmute.'

Karmi Hatu nodded in agreement with Sagan's explanation.

I just do not know what Shu-ilishu was telling the merchant of Sumer who had perhaps accumulated copper, tin and zinc in the three pots kept behind the stool on which the merchant sat.

'What was hidden in a foundation pot of the ziggurat? What minerals were used to create the foundation for Ea's temple?'

My questions would not cease.

Sagan just smiled. Karmi Hatu also smiled. The smile reminded me of the smile on the bronze dancing girl's pouted lips.

I will not be able to erase her image from the memories of my brain, not in this life-time. Her image, her every dance step is ingrained like the cosmic dance steps of Śiva-Naṭarāja. Now he sits in meditation on the summit of Mount Kailas allowing the waters to melt from the glaciers of Manasarovar in Tibet.

That great physicist Newton believed in alchemy. Were the physicists of CERN watched by Śiva-Naṭarāja's bronze every day of their lives also like Newton, believers in the relativity of subatomic particles with the molecules of DNA chains?

I asked Ashutosh a Ph.D student in Physics in University of Maryland. He confirmed that transmutation of all elements in the periodic table was possible. What was needed was energy in abundance to achieve the transmutation.

Was the energy of the incessant fire of five days and nights in a *soma yajña*, together with the alchemical concoction in Karmi Hatu's *kamaṇḍalu* adequate to achieve the transmutation? Who knows?

I was not sure if Shu-ilishu's language skills could adequately communicate to the Sumer merchant, the mysteries contained in Karmi Hatu's pot.

Sagan and Karmi Hatu were on a life's journey which was, like pilgrim's progress, a search for Sarasvati.

We do not even know when the dynamic Himalaya will stop rumbling with the perpetual tectonic eruptions. These tectonics have to continue to sustain the lives of millions of people dependent upon the fresh water flowing from the Himalayan glaciers.

Newton has to become a hydrologist to create an Indian Ocean Community the way the two world wars created a European Community, an entity celebrated with a Nobel Peace Prize. The prize is an affirmation of Rāṣṭram, an abiding union of nations of people, served by *ambhas*, water. So goes the tradition of offering water ablutions as the fire blazes near Sagan's anvil in his brass foundry.

Sagan also collects herbals which act as क्षार *kṣāra* salts to remove the oxides from the minerals. We just have to wonder at *Paramātman*'s creation of wonders of phenomena in this physical world of subatomic particles and molecules of DNA. All barriers between physics and genetics have to be broken to unravel the mysteries of *Parabrahman* that celestial, metaphysical *ātman*.

The story of Sagan's life has a happy ending. Sagan keeps smiling even as he sweats beating the brass plate to shape on the anvil with Karmi Hatu's help. She is his *śakti*, the primordial prowess, his wife, female divinity. She is at times angry, like *āsurī Sarasvatī*.

Sagan told me once, 'I got the techniques of mixing correct proportions of copper and zinc from my Assur ancestor's knowledge of metals. Yes, the same Assur who made the non-rusting Delhi iron pillar.'

Archaeologist Jarrige found at Nausharo, Mehergarh, two female terracotta figurines. Period 1B, 2800 – 2600 BCE. 11.6 x 30.9 cm. Hair is painted black and parted in the middle of the forehead, with traces of red pigment in the part.This

form of ornamentation may be the origin of the later Hindu tradition where a married woman wears a streak of vermilion or powdered cinnabar (sindur) in the part of her hair. Choker and pendant necklace are also painted with red pigment, posssibly to represent carnelian beads.

Sagan asked Karmi, 'Did you learn the art of wearing vermilion in the parting of your hair from this Sarasvati?'

Karmi replied like Vāk, with an emphatic, 'Yes.'

This is the story of Sagan and Karmi. Every love story has a happy ending.

Sagan finds Sarasvati.

Chapter 16 *Bos indicus* as hieroglyph

I told Sagan, 'I do not propose to offer a decipherment for the corpora of Indus script.'

Sagan raised his voice to an assertive tone, 'Do not try to hide from reality. You have to explain the thousands of seals and tablets including copper plates with inscriptions. Most of them may relate to the language of Sarasvati's children. We are searching for Sarasvati and we have to provide leads the way Father Brown would have done. He is our detective model.'

'Yes, we have dealt with *Anser indicus*. We have also done detective work on Soma of Vedic language. Let us move on to *Bos indicus*.'

There are at least two clear depictions of bulls on Indus corpora. One is of *Bos indicus*, the other of a bull calf ligatured with one horn and a pannier. Of course, there is a standard device shown often in front of the bull calf. Let us start with naming the *Bos indicus* and the bull calf.

We are not yet in a position to name the Meluhha merchant carrying the antelope shown on Shu-ilishu Akkadian cuneiform cylinder seal.

But, the Indus script corpora and archaeological reports demonstrate that 80 percent of the archaeological sites are on the banks of Sarasvati River system.

My Indus lexicon has shown the essential semantic continuum evidenced by over 25 ancient Indian languages.

We can justify the use of some of these lexemes to read the inscriptions, because we have, following Father Brown's success in identifying the postman, demonstrated the dynamic Himalayas, locus of sites like Bhirrana, Kalibangan on the banks of Sarasvati River system emanating from the Himalayas and the meaning of Soma in Vedic language as the Vedic people performed Soma yajña all along the River Basin as shown by Balarama's visit to the *āśrama* of many Rishis on his Sarasvati pariyātra described in the Śalya parva of the Great Epic.

So, let us start with some clues as Father Brown would have done.

A bull calf is shown on over 1100 Indus inscriptions.

Bos indicus, also called zebu is a hieroglyph which occurs on over 50 Indus inscriptions included in Indus script corpora.

The majesty of this animal is brought out with extraordinary care on many inscriptions.

Elementary, Father Brown. The glyphs are category markers, marking categories central to the life-activities of Sarasvati's children who were nurtured on her banks.

Bos indicus and the bull calf denote two categories of production-facilities: 1. Furnace. 2. Workshop.

Fish, arrow and four short-strokes denote two categories of resources used: 1. Metal. 2. Charaterisation of the metal.

Inscriptions are composed of glyphs. Clues emerge by matching lexemes with the orthography.

Let us start with the two samples of *Bos indicus* seals.

Three glyphs:

ayo 'fish' (Munda) +

kaṇḍa 'arrow' (Sanskrit)

gaṇḍa four' (Munda) [Note: four short strokes is an allograph for arrow, hence both are phonetic cognates.]

Read together, the glyphs connote: *ayo kaṇḍa*

The combined reading ayaskāṇḍa means, 'a quantity of iron, excellent iron' (according to Panini, the grammarian) *kāṇḍa* means, 'furnace metal.'

> Cognates: काण्डः kāṇḍḥ ण्डम् ṇḍam A cluster, bundle, multitude. An arrow.
>
> काण्ड *m.* (also) abundance, Vcar. *mfn.* a multitude , heap , quantity (ifc.) *mfn.* काण्ड्/अ any part or portion , section , chapter , division of a work or book (cf. त्रि-क्°) *mfn.* a separate department or subject (e.g. कर्म-काण्ड , the department of the वेदtreating of sacrificial rites.

The glyph of *Bos indicus* or zebu:

khũṭ 'zebu' (Kathiawar Gujarati)

> Cognates: *khũṭro* entire bull used for agriculture, not for breeding (Gujarati); *khunṭiyo* an uncastrated bull (Kathiawad. Gujarati) *khũ_ṭaḍum* a bullock (used in Jhālwāḍ)(Gujarati) *kuṇṭai* bull (Tamil) *khũdhi* hump on the back; *khuĩ_dhũ* hump-backed (Gujarati)

A similar sounding word *kuṭi* means 'smelting furnace' (Munda)

> Cognate words are: *kuṭhi, kuṭi* (Or.; Sad. koṭhi) (1) the smelting furnace of the blacksmith; *kuṭire bica duljaḍko talkena*, they were feeding the furnace with ore; (2) the name of *ēkuṭi* has been given to the fire which, in lac factories, warms the water bath for softening the lac so that it can be spread into sheets; to make a smelting furnace; *kuṭhi-o* of a smelting furnace, to be made; the smelting furnace of the blacksmith is made of mud, cone-shaped, 2' 6" dia. At the base and 1' 6" at the top. The hole in the center, into which the mixture of charcoal and iron ore is poured, is about 6" to 7" in dia. At the base it has two holes, a smaller one into which the nozzle of the bellow is inserted, and a larger one on the

opposite side through which the molten iron flows out into a cavity (Munda).

Semantic expansion: *kūṭa* a house, dwelling (Sanskrit.lex.) *khũṭ* = a community, sect, society, division, clique, schism, stock; *khũṭren peṛa kanako* they belong to the same stock (Santali) *khũṭ* Nag. *khũṭ, kūṭ* Has. (Or. *khũṭ*) either of the two branches of the village family. *kūṭa* joining, connexion, assembly, crowd, fellowship. Pali. *gotta* 'clan'; Prakrit. *gotta, gōya* id.

Apart from the line of glyphs on top and standard device in front, three ligaturing glyphs clearly constitute the orthographically elaborated bull calf:

1. Bull calf
2. Pannier, sometimes rings on neck
3. One horn:

A young bull is *kōḍe, khōṇḍa*

Cognates: *koḍiyum koḍiyum* 'bull calf' (Gujarati) *kāru-kōḍe* [Telugu] n. A bull in its prime. [*kōḍiya*] Gujarati *godhɔ* m. bull ', *godhũ* n. young bull ', Old Gujarati *godhalu* m. entire bull ', Gujarati godhliyũ n. young bull ' Telugu. *kōḍiya, kōḍe* young bull; adj. male (e.g. *kōḍe dūḍa* bull calf), young, youthful; *kōḍekāḍu* a young man. Kol. (Haig) *kōḍē* bull. Nk. *khoṛe* male calf. Konḍa *kōḍi* cow; *kōṛe* young bullock. Pe. *kōḍi* cow. Manḍ. *kūḍi* id. Kui kōḍi id., ox. Kuwi (F.) *kōdi* cow; (S.) *kajja kōḍi* bull ; (Su. P.) *kōḍi* cow cf. *koṛa* 'a boy, a young man' (Santali)

koḍiyum 'rings on neck' (Gujarati) *koṭiyum* = a wooden circle put round the neck of an animal; *koṭ* = neck (Gujarati)

One horn is *koḍ, kōṇḍa* Pa. *kōḍ* (pl. *kōḍul*) horn; Ka. *kōḍu*

Cognates: *kōṟ* horn Tu. *kōḍů, kōḍu* horn Ko. *kṛ* (obl. *kṭ-*)(Paš. *kōṇḍā* 'bald', Kal. rumb. *kōṇḍa* 'hornless'. Kal. rumb. *khōṇḍ* a' half'.

A sack slung on the front shoulder of the young bull is *khōṇḍā, khōṇḍī, kothḷɔ* खोंडा [*khōṇḍā*] m A कांबळा of which one end is formed into a cowl or hood. खोंडी [*khōṇḍī*] f An outspread shovelform sack (as formed temporarily out of a कांबळा, to hold or fend off grain, chaff. (Marathi) *khŏdrang, khudrang* ख्वद्ंरंग adj. c.g. self-coloured; as subst. m. N. of a kind of blanket having the natural colour of the wool (L. 37).

Similar sounding words: *koḍ* 'workshop' (Kuwi.Gujarati) *kŭdār* 'turner' (Bengali)

Father Brown would have said: Not many people notice a postman nowadays. History is all around us, the words spoken by our ancestors who wrote in Indus script are all around us and part of our identity.

A clue has been found, the glyphs of inscriptions are category markers.

Has the script been deciphered?

As the Vedic rishi would ask, "who knows?"

Sagan Munda and Karmi Hatu were simply playing with the *Anser indicus* pair feeding from the grains spread out to dry. Who knows? They may be a pair of *paramahamsa.*

Chapter 17 Sagan and Father Brown: An inquisition

Sagan was no ornithologist, he was not an expert who could identify subspecies of *Anser indicus*.

He said, with finality in his voice, 'You have to make your thesis falsifiable. That is the benchmark of *satyam,* 'truth' which academia will look at even without footnotes.'

Sagan continued, 'Father Brown may be an adequate role model for identifying qualifications one looks for before selecting C.I.A. agents or 007 operatives or para-psychologists who will fathom what the enemies in Russia or China are scheming. But, in your case, you have to explain in a footnote the famous controversy which arose in an Ivy League Parker University.'

Sagan was referring to the controversy about awarding Ph.D. to an archaeology student who had transgressed into language studies. The chairman of the thesis committee rejected Bruce's thesis pronouncing with an assurance, 'The thesis is too argumentative. There can't be any decipherment on a non-writing system by illiterates. All glyphs on inscriptions of Indus script corpora are doodles. You have failed to provide a falsifiable basis for the Dissertation Committee to accept that they are not doodles, that they are not fakes or forgeries. You have failed the Fathrr Brown test of a true detective.'

The dean of the Archaeoogy department was a compassionate academician who had studied the Iranian languages and seen the Egyptian hieroglyphs deciphered successfully by Champollion. He tried to plead for Bruce because he felt responsible for leading Bruce into a blind alley by suggesting decipherment of Indus glyphs as a fit enough subject for a thesis of publishable quality standards of the prestigious Parker University.

The chairman relented and recommended acceptance of Bruce's thesis, though tentative, though non-falsifiable, for calling Bruce a Doctor of Philosophy.

The story of the controversy became the topic of discussion in Saffron which is the Students' magazine of the University. Reports began to appear on news media. The reports never reached talk shows on Television channels.

Sagan intervened as I continued the Bruce narrative, 'See, the real problem is the absence of a jury. Father Brown never had to contend with a jury. His detective work attained fame because the criminals accepted their crimes and surrendered to the police.'

'So what is to be done?' I was perplexed, not knowing how to proceed further with my earth-shaking theses on *Bos indicus* without producing a Rosetta stone. The academics will reject inscriptions on birch barks as modern fakes showing Indus script glyphs at random and call them gibberish, not a record of the teachings of the Buddha, the Enlightened One.

What do we do? Is there someone who can help me? I don't want any Ph.D. degree. I just want to tell the avid readers of detective stories that there is a method which links Indus script and Egyptian hieroglyphs which have been accepted as a writing system.

Sagan came up with an idea. He took me to Tchakovsky, the conductor of the famed Bonn Philharmonic Orchestra.

Tchakovsky said, 'I am no ornithologist to narrate the 20-year life story of monogamous *Anser indicus*. It is amazing that they should evince such fidelity in married life. Surely, they should have ways of identifying each other and recognizing their goslings. I do not know if the crackling sounds produced by the monogamous pair are unique enough to be distinguished from quacks of ducks using diagnostic audiometers used to evaluate hearing loss in humans.'

Sagan responded, 'Tchakovsky, I can take you to my brass foundry. In front of my house, a pair of *Anser indicus* has been visiting every winter with an astonishing regularity. Maybe they fly in from Kyrgyzstan across Mount Kailas. I can record their crackles and the crackles of their goslings and bring them to you.'

Tchakovsky was not convinced, 'Who am I to behave like a musicologist? I think we have to set up a jury composed of recognized experts from a very wide range of academic disciplines. That is the only way either *Nature* or *Scientific American* magazine will accept a letter for publication. We should also include a journalist specializing in archaeology as a member of the jury.'

Sagan nodded in agreement, adding, 'I was privileged to get the permission of the Lahore Museum curator to blow into the conch kept in the museum. I will blow into it to prove to you. It produces the primordial sound, OM which in tradition is called a form of the Supreme Divine, *paramātman*. I thik museums should not merely exhibit such conches but also allow them to be blown into by museum visitors.'

Tchakovsky's orchestra cannot replicate the OM sound produced by the 3 millennia old conch of Lahore Museum. I will just show you a photograph of the conch, dated in an archaeological context, provenance, to circa 3rd millennium BCE. Two such conch shells excavated from Harappa are also shown in the British Library's India Office Select Materials catalog.

I told Tchakovsky, 'I will blow the Lahore Museum conch which makes the sound OM. It ain't no fake. Which jury will sit in judgement over the meaning of the sound which emanates from the 3 millennia-old conch?'

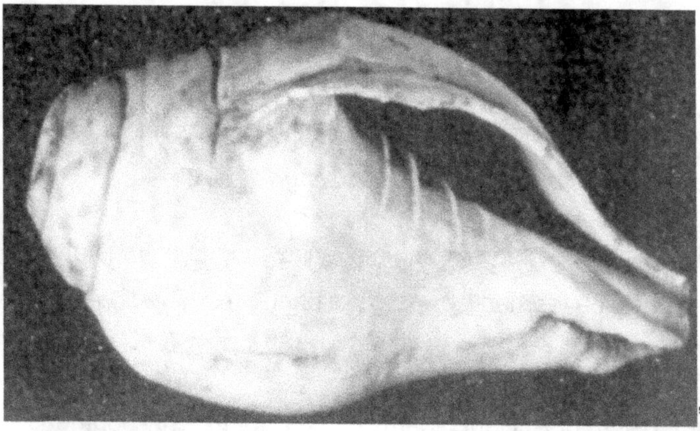

' *Turbinella pyrum* conch shell trumpet. Hole at apex is roughly chipped. Used to call people for battle or ritually for prayers, throughout South and Southeast Asia. Essential component of Hindu and Buddhist traditions, one of 8 auspicious symbols. 9.66 X 5.1 cm. Harappa; Lahore Museum, P501.

This reminds us of the *Pāñcajanya* of Kṛṣṇa.

I have taken care to provide the Museum Acquisition Number so that it will be acceptable as evidence in a court of law. I have also taken care to use the high-sounding Latin name calling it *turbinella pyrum* to sound authentic, to the scientific community which looks for falsifiable hypotheses.

A seal cut out of conch shell, excavated at Dwaraka.

Two swastika seals exhibited in the British Museum

'All this is anecdotal evidence, not enough to prove your thesis,' said Tchakovsky as he lapsed into an introspective mood, took the violin in his hands and rendered an octave, 'Sure, I cannot produce the sound of *that* conch shell. I can only come close to it'.

‘The way to put together a jury,’ Sagan explained, ‘is to assemble expert musicologists, ornithologists and doctors who can study the bizarre monogamous behavior of *Anser indicus*. But, then, how do you allow skeptical scholars to falsify your decoding of fish as *aya* and not *carp* or *salmon*?’

‘Good questions’, I said as the professors would say answering questions about their presentation at the end of a learned symposium, during the question-answer session.

‘Aha, why not call a symposium of Ancient Near East and South Asia-Southeast Asia experts so that they can be given the responsibility of selecting a 10-member jury from among themselves?’

‘Should we drag the issue to a criminal court, as if it is a cognizable crime of murder?’ I asked.

‘Yes,’ said Sagan emphatically, ‘this has to be a criminal trial. Any other forum will allow reporters continue allegations about forgery or production of false sounds, making them sound like OM.’

‘I will prove my case from the received wisdom of Egyptian hieroglyphs. Here it is, a sample of hieroglyphs which name Emperor Narmer.’

This Narmer Palette also known as the Great Hierakonopolis Palette is an archaeological find dated to circa 31st century BCE. Both sides of the Palette show the pair of hieroglyphs enclosed in a *serekh* flanked by two horned heads of bulls, indicating that the reference is to an emperor who was uniting Upper and Lower Egypt. A facsimile of the Palette is on display at the Royal Ontario Museum in Toronto, Canada.

I am told by Egyptologists like Sazzon that the Palette which is large and heavy was not used for personal use but was deployed to grind cosmetics to adorn the statues of Divinities.

This is an amazing pattern of creating images of Divinities, as metaphysical forces beyond the physical or material phenomena.

Let us look at an enlarged drawing of the *serekh* on the Palette. Egyptologist Bob Brier has referred to the Narmer Palette as 'the first historical document in the world.' Maybe, at the about the same time, that is around 33rd century BCE, artisans of Sarasvati River basin were using hieroglyphs on seals.

A *serekh* (like the cartouche to name Cleopatra) encloses two glyphs. One glyph is a catfish shown horizontally on the top register. The second glyph is a chisel shown vertically in the bottom register. (Note that the chisel is almost comparable to the gimlet shown in front of the bull calf, the gimlet is called a 'standard device' by analysts of Indus script corpora.)

The catfish is: /n'>r/

The chisel is: /mr/

Read together, we get the vocalized name assuming some that vowels existed between consonants: Narmer.

The Dean of Archaeology Department of Parker University agreed to co-chair with Tchakovsky, the international Ancient Near East-South Asia-Southeast Asia Symposium. It was a unique pairing of a Conductor of Bonn Philharmonic Orchestrar and a Dean of an Ivy League University.

The symposium is yet to be scheduled.

But, the criminal trial proceeded in a US Superior court.

Sarsuti was the judge. She approved the selection of 10-member jury to whom I presented the following summation as the leading advocate in the criminal case.

'Brothers and sisters', I started, the way Swami Vivekananda addressed the World Parliament of Religions. I owe no apology for shamelessly plagiarizing Swami's words.

'Objection, Judge Sarsuti, the defense attorney is using emotional appeals in what should be a scientifically proven case,' thundered the Prosecutor who had charged Sagan with the criminal charge of forgery.

'Brothers and sisters,' I continued since Honorable Judge Sarsuti did not demur.

I sum up my case in defense of Sagan with the confidence that you will endorse *satyam* that primordial principle which governs all our lives together with *ṛta* and *dharma*.

At the outset, I should clear the doctrine of laches. In Greek mythology, Lachesis was the second of the Three Fates, normally clothed like Sarasvati in white robes. Lachesis measured the thread woven by Clotho's spindle and determined the thread of life. Lachesis was the apportioner of infinite time, determining the time for life permitted for each one of us as human beings. The Doctrine of Laches derives from the functions of Lachesis to determine if a case should be declared time-barred in jurisprudence.

I submit, Honorable MadamJudge, my revered Jury members, that the Doctrine of Laches should not apply in this case, though we have produced evidence dated to 6500 BCE and to 31st century BCE in the case of Narmer Palette and to 33rd century BCE in the case of Harappa potsherd with Indus script inscription. The Doctrine is not applicable because Adolf Hitler abused, in the 20th century CE, the glyph of Indus script corpora, the swastika beyond its true function, which was simply used as a hieroglyph to denote zinc mineral worked on by brass-workers like my client, Sagan.

Zinc was called *jasta* in Meluhha, the way Sarasvati was called Sarsuti in Meluhha. *Jasta* as a phonetic transform of *svastika* was permitted use in Meluhha semantics. *Jasta* like *svastika* had the meaning of 1. a non-metallic mineral, zinc and 2. graphic form svastika. As proof, I can cite a cognate semantic of a Kannada word: *satthiya* which means 'pewter (an alloy of copper antimony, bismuth and tin)'. Actually, the word pewter is a variant of the word spelter which is a term for zinc alloy or zinc itself. One group of people spoke with correct pronunciation of the word Sarasvati, another group abbreviated the pronunciation to *Sarsuti.* This is the reason why some channels shown the Survey of India atlases show the name of channels as Sarsuti while they, in fact, were channels of Sarasvati River system.

This is why I refer to Honorable Judge Sarsuti as an embodiment of Devi Sarasvati come to judgement. I am not getting emotional. I am stating a semantic fact of phonetic transformations to carry meaning through the typical characterists of language evolution and change.

In the Indian tradition also, there is a Lachesis. He is called Citragupta who assists as a record keeper for Yama. We can say that Citragupta is the original script-writer shown on Indus script with the 'rim of jar' glyph. The rim of jar in Meluhha is called *kanka* as in Santali. The same rim of jar in Prakrit language is called *karṇaka* Both relate to the same orthography, the rim of the narrow-necked jar. The word kanka has two meanings: one is 'rim of jar'. The other is 'scribe', like the scribes who prepared tallies and bullaes in Susa to keep accounts of the material resources used by temple-workers. In the Indus script corpora, many tablets serve the functions similar to those served by Sumerian or Elamite tallies and bullae. Tablets were used by artisans working on circular platforms to deliver specific products and resources into the warehouse. Seals recorded these artisan tallies to be handed over to the seafaring merchant. The task was performed by the scribe, *kanka.* This explains why the hieroglyph of 'rim of jar' which reads *kanka* is the most frequently-occurring glyph on Indus script corpora.

That svastika glyph refers to zinc as a mineral can be seen from two evidences: 1. The evidene of svastika seal excavated in Altyn-depe; and 2. The evidence of

one side of a three-sided prism tablet which shows svastika embedded in a *serekh* (almost like a cartouche), flanked by an elephant and a tiger. We know that elephant refers to *ib, ibha* ‘elephant’ which is a hieroglyph to denote a similar sounding word *ib*, ‘iron’ in Meluhha. Ib is also the name of a Railway station on the Mumbai-Howrah route. Ib is close to Bokaro steel plant. We also know that tiger refers to *kol, kul* as a hieroglyph to denote a similar sounding word *kol*, ‘iron’. What the lexicons refer to as ‘iron’ may refer in earlier times to ‘a hard, stony metal’. The word *kollan* meaning ‘smith’, for example, comes from this word *kol*, ‘iron’, though the ‘smith’ dealt with many metals including iron. The person seated on the tree next to the tiger is, like Sagan, an inquirer. Sometimes texts refer to him as *heraka*, ‘spy’. A similar sounding word *eraka* means ‘copper’. Thus, we have on this side of the tablet, a list of metallic and non-metallic minerals used by brass-workers like Sagan. From left to right, the list includes: *ib,* ‘iron’; *satthiya* ‘zinc or maybe, pewter’; *kol*, ‘iron’; *eraka* ‘copper’.

I invite attention of Honorable Judge Sarsuti and Members of the Jury to the most emphatic evidence conclusively proving the meaning of ‘fish’ hieroglyph as a reference to *aya,* ‘metal’. This evidence corroborates the evidence of ‘fish’ glyph show on the Susa pot which contained metal tools and weapons.

I wil just cite the evidence of two tablets which show a gharial (alligator) catching

a fish in its jaws. There are about 50 such tablets and seals depicting a gharial. It is also sometimes referred to as Gangetic gharial.

Ayaskāra is a compound attested in Panini, like Narmer attested on the Egyptian Palette. *Ayaskāra* a synonym of *loha-kāra* means‘metalsmith or metal artisan’

(Sanskrit).A cognate word *kāruvu* means mechanic, artisan. *Aya* means 'fish'; also 'metal' (Munda). *kāru* means 'crocodile' (Telugu). Combing the two rods, denoted by fish and crocodile, *ayakāra* means 'ironsmith' (Pali).

Now, have I not submitted a falsifiable hypothesis that the fish glyph should in ALL contexts of the Indus corpora refer to metal which was called *aya* or *ayo* or *ayas* in many Indian languages ?

Brothers and sisters, sympathize with my predicament. Unlike Father Brown who was only a detective who would hand over the killer or murderer to the police to continue with the prosecution in a court of law, Sagan has to perform his role not only as a detective but as a defendant who has to engage a criminal lawyer to prove his detective work in a court of law. Thus, Sagan is performing the roles of Father Brown and Inspector Poirot. It is travesty of justice to charge him with forgery for his failure to copy the two short-strokes which were shown on a tablet on top of a jar glyph. The two short-strokes flanking both sides of the mouth of the jar are a very important orthographic feature in Indus script corpora. The strokes signified that the artist was trying to convey not the 'jar' word but the word for the 'rim of the jar.' Sagan has proved his honesty by obtaining the trademark patent for his Jagadhri brasspot which is world-renowned.

Sagan's failure in reproducing the two short strokes has now been remedied by the use of new technology to produce authentic transcripts from the original seal or tablet. This new technology renders the charge of forgery meaningless, because this trial, in its essence, is about 'meaning' which is central to any linguistic argument. Both the sender and the recipient of the message have to understand the 'meaning' conveyed is the same. In the case of the 'forged' document produced by the Prosecution, the Meluhha merchant and the Akkadian buyer clearly understood that the 'rim of jar' even with hazy two-strokes on one side or either side of the mouth of the jar did not incidate the word *kanka*. The seal was understood by the buyer to have come from Meluhha scribe. There is no other writing system for any language anywhere on the globe which uses a rim of jar glyph to denote *kanka*, scribe. At this stage, I should remind the Jury about another meaning assigned to Sarasvati. She is also called Vāk, she is recognized in tradition to have embodied sacred speech, the Word. Can anyone claim that the Vedic language was forged when the word Vāk is used for Vāgāmbhriṇī or Sarasvati? No one would ever doubt that the word Sarasvati also referred to a mighty Himalayan river.

Metaphor is the culprit, Honorable Judge Sarsuti.

Again, reverting to the Doctrine of Laches, we are not submitting our case for the Honorable Court to arbitrate on the dispute on the relative chronology of Narmer Palette dated to 31st century BCE, while the Indus script origin is dated to circa 33rd century BCE because we have no knowledge or evidence for a chronology of many priest-kings of the civilization on the banks of River Sarasvati, unlike the situation on the banks of River Nile. We are only submitting for your considered judgement and award that if laches do not apply to Narmer, laches should not also apply to hundreds of thousands of *ayakāra,* who like Sagan, are metal-workers, even today. In summary, *ayakāra* are a living phenomena amidst us, Sarasvati has decided to flow again on the land as the Jury members had witnessed at Gedra Road and hence, the Doctrine of Laches should NOT apply in this case.

Honorable Judge Sarsuti and Honored Members of the Jury, I also submit that my client is innocent and is merely an inquirer like that Ph.D student of Parker University. My client should not be subjected to harsh judgement or harsh punishment for trying to bring before the reading public the Song of the monogamous pair of *Anser indicus*. We have produced the testimony of Tchakovsky, an eminent conductor of Bonn Philharmonic Orchestra. He has emphatically stated, as an expert in music, that it is impossible to reproduce the tone and rhythm of the primordial sound OM of human voice rendered through the blow of the breath of life from one's being through the sacred conch, *śankha*, on any human-made musical instrument.

On a personal note, I submit to you as a servant of the Law that we are all together in this historic case which re-opens the PEEM (Parents for Equalization of Education Materials) case in the United States District Court of the Eastern District of California on the famous Harvard Donkey Trial.

It was a major victory for PEEM when the Judge rejected the defendants' motion to dismiss PEEM's law suit to correct inaccuracies in sixth grade history textbooks. PEEM's complaint contends that the process to adopt the textbooks discriminated against Hindus and that the textbooks indulge in indoctrination of foreign religious notions while using disparaging language against Hinduism. The Judge noted that the PEEM's claim that the defendants conducted the process of adoption of textbooks that was discriminatory.

Unfortunately, that case did not get to the trial phase of putting defendants on the witness box and to the final judgement phase because of a good-faith settlement. The Honorable Court has rendered the settlement without prejudice, implying that this Honorable Judge Sarsuti Court has jurisdiction to render a judgement which will also have an impact on follow-up action on the Harvard Donkey case.

I should digress and remind the Jury about the reason why the case which was dealt with by a settlement and still open for final adjudication by this Honorable Court, was called Harvard Donkey case. The name comes because a Harvard Professor had famously stated what were claimed to be horses by Hindus in India were donkeys. The discovery process during the trial proved that this claim was made in order to push a mythical Caphetic Race Theory into textbooks. The famous case thus was in the continuum of cases pitting science against creationism. Hindus were on the side of science, while the learned professor was on the side of creationism.

The present court, I submit with all humility and whatever learning imparted to me in the learned schools of law of the land, is like a spark from the anvil of the International Court Justice. We are dealing with sparks from the anvil when we deal with the life-views formed in a formative age in middle-school children about our civilizational heritage. It is our collective dharma, responsibility, to undo the damage done by untruths – *asatyam* -- contained in California and other State textbooks. In this case, Sagan is not the only accused facing trial as a defendant, defending the absolute and eternal right to truth.

The other, invisible, unnamed accused is history of a civilization which has been injured by the charge of illiteracy for our ancestors.

Were the artisans who made Narmer Palette illiterate? If NOT, the artisans who made the inscriptions now cataloged in Indus script corpora are as literate as the carvers of the Narmer Palette.

I stand before you submitting this to the amorphous, undefinable, indeterminate, nameless court of history.

We cannot allow our children to be misled with *asatyam*, falsehoods. Am I getting repetitive and emotional or political here? I submit, certainly not. I am only adding emphasis, asking the Jury and this Honorable Court to pronounce the truth.

Learned Prosecutor has produced the conch seal of Dwaraka and challenged the Defense to prove the meaning of three heads of animals ligatured to a bovine body: the heads of a bull, a bull calf and an antelope like the one carried by the Meluhhan merchant interpreted by Shu-ilishu Akkadian or Sumerian interpreter. Here are the answers approved -- by shouting OM of endorsement in unison -- by the international symposium of academicians and journalist-reporters on archaeology, music, geology, remote sensing and other subjects based on the evidence of a Mesopotamian cuneiform text we have produced before the Court.

I should add that the latest state-of-the-art Reflectance Imaging Technology (RTI) wad deployed to detect the two short-strokes on the seal which showed the jar, the only piece of evidence cited by the Prosecution to charge my client Sagan for criminal negligence on such a document of vital importance to determine our roots, the roots of our civilization. The Jury Members will be happy to note that the same Reflectance Imaging Technology is deployed to decipher the tough

Proto-Elamite writing system. No one has so far accused the Proto-Elamite who wrote the tablets with the charge of illiteracy.

Permit me to read from the consensus opinion of scholars of Code of Hammurabi:

> '2 mina of silver (the value of): 5 gur of oil (and of) 30 garments for an expedition to Telmun to buy (there) copper, (as the) capital for a partnership, L. and N. have borrowed from U. After safe termination of the voyage, he (the creditor) will not recognize commercial losses (incurred by the debtor); they (the debtors) have agreed to satisfy U (the creditor) with 4 mina of copper for each shekel of silver as a just (price(?)].'.. babitum must denote some kind of customs or dues imposed on the merchants by the city administration... all extant Old and Neo-Babylonian contracts on partnership reserve for the tamkarum not only the invested capital (plus interest) but also an equal share of the profit yielded by the business venture... The complex legal relationship between the investing and the travelling merchant has created a number of loan types of which at least two are mentioned in the Code of Hammurabi. One of them uses the characteristic term tadmiqtu. We encounter this word in the paragraphs 102-103 of the Code and in a few documents of that period..."

Doctrine of *res judicata* mandates this Honorable Court to enforce the Code of Hammurabi bypassing any doctrinal interpretation of Laches.

The three heads of animals sanctified on the Dwaraka seal carved out on a fragment of sacred conch refer to the legal, contractual relationship between three groups of professionals, a contract consistent with the Code of Hammurabi:

Professional No. 1 *ḍangar* 'bull'; read rebus: *tamkarum* 'merchant'; cognate: *ṭhākur* 'blacksmith '(Maithili); lord, title (Sanskrit)

Professional No. 2 *koḍe*, 'bull calf'; *koḍ* 'one horn' read rebus: *koḍ* 'workshop'; *khōṇḍī* 'pannier' read rebus: *kũdār* 'turner' (Bengali)

Professional No. 3 *mr̤eka* 'goat, antelope' read rebus *meṛh* 'helper of merchant' *milakkhu* 'copper'.

Now, I can submit to the Honorable Court that the Meluhhan carrying a goat was in fact announcing his profession as 'helper of copper merchant'. That he was a Meluhhan was announced by the rebus word: *meṛh* connoted by *mr̤eka* 'goat, antelope'. It is surprising that the merchant did NOT announce his name but only stated his profession. It is a characteristic humility of the Sarasvati's children of ancient times.

Now, I am in a position to refute the arguments of the Prosecutor who challenged me to decipher

1) two Kalibangan seals showing an antelope and a fish glyph; and

2) a seal in the National Museum, Delhi (perhaps from Mohenjodaro Acquisition Number 135) showing two heads of bull and bull calf on a bovine body together with a fish glyph.

I am extremely grateful to the Prosecutor for assisting the Honorable Court with these three important inscriptions from the Indus script corpora, which I submit constitute my central and fundamental submission. As noted about the glyph of zebu almost all the glyphs of the Indus script are category indicators.

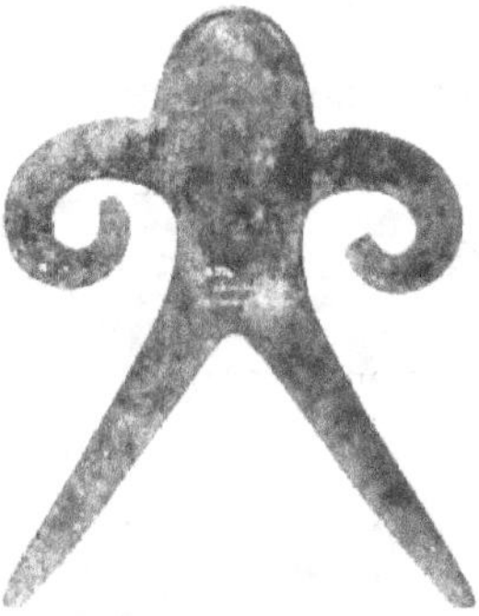

Zebu was an indicator of technological production facility of the metal work factory of the smith-community, sometimes also called a smithy.

The other animals were specific professional work-assignments in a smithy related to particular resources such as metallic minerals, non-metallic minerals and metals, for example iron ore (elephant), iron (tiger), antelope (helper of copper merchant), bull calf (workshop turner, sometimes also called a forge or foundry -- like my client Sagan's brass foundry).

I submit, Honorable Judge and Revered Members of the Jury that the fish glyph continues to denote the category of *aya* 'metal, an alloy of copper and tin creating bronze or of copper and zinc creating brass).

This is also the explanation for the inscription of only the fish glyph on a copper anthropomorphs now kept in many Indian museums. Reflectance Imaging Technology has not shown any other glyph on the body of the anthropomorph.

Copper anthropomorph with 'fish' glyph incised on the chest. The horns of a markhor are humanized like curved arms. This particular evidence comes from Sheorajpur, Kanpur District, Uttar Pradesh, India and is kept in the Lucknow Museum. Such anthropomorphs are typical finds in Gangetic copper hoards. *meḍho* a ram, a sheep (Gujarati) read rebus *meḍ* iron (Ho.) meṛh 'helper of copper merchant', that is, a metalsmith artisan smith working in the merchant's smithy.

The seals produced as evidence of doodles by the Prosecutor, in fact, turn out to be consistent with the rebus readings which follow the method used also on Egyptian hieroglyphs which were successfully deciphered by Champollion.

I have to remind the Members of the Jury of the famous quote of Father Brown 'Nobody ever notices postmen somehow.' The exquisite glyphs on the entire Indus Script corpora are such unnoticed postmen who conveyed the messages using the famous Narmer technique of hieroglyphic writing system.

Father Brown noticed a postman's bag and realized how the bag was used to carry the dead body, after committing a crime.

In this case in which Sagan, who, assisted by Karmi Hatu has produced trademark Jagadhri brass pots and other vessels used in millions of households the world over, has committed no crime.

On the contrary, he and Karmi Hatu should be complimented by the Revered Jury for reinforcing the primacy of work in our lives. My client, Sagan, with the assistance of Karmi Hatu has led an exemplary life as an artisan and carried on the flag of tradition of *dharma* enunciated by our elders, our ancestors.

All of us owe our very identity to the elders and ancestors.

In a way, Sagan trial is a reminder and a continuation of the PEEM Harvard Donkey case. This trial is, in fact, a *śrāddham* as a *samskāra* we are performing together as a family united in jurisprudence and the Rule of Law. This is a historic case, Honorable Judge. I rest my case. The Jury is still out.

Chapter 18 Karmi Hatu, Sarsuti

I refer to Sarsuti, Meluhha name for Sarasvati.

Karmi Hatu continued my summing-up arguments which ha become the talk of the town .

Some parents who are members of PEEM and one Archaeology reporter asked for my interview.

The Defendant Counsel's summing-up was cited even on a CNN International talk-show as a stunning narrative history of seven millennia.

I heard reports that a Hollywood Director who was fascinated by the famous *Schindler's List* and had directed the *Life of Shey* showed interest in making a movie using the story-line. One consultant listed on the *Literary Marketplace* called me up to ask if I would be interested in selling the rights to re-format the illustrated novel into a screen-play and asked for an additional list of resource persons such as para-psychologists working with satellite images to unravel secret designs of America's enemies in Russia and China, who should be included in the cast. I told the consultant that the cast is already long enough for the story to be told on the silver screen or even on a High Definition Movie distributed through cable and satellite TV channels with simultaneous release all over the world.

Karmi Hatu continued, 'The discovery of Sarasvati get defined by an extraordinary tablet recently excavated from Harappa by the Harvard multi-disciplinary team. I refer to the so-called copper tablet in bas-relief with raised script. Actually, it is not a copper tablet but an unusual alloy of copper, lead, zinc without antimony, a sort of zinc-pewter.'

Karmis showed me the photograph of the tablet. The centerpiece is the human back-bone glyph. Hamavedan has proved that this is a variant glyph of a kneeling adorant. The glyph reads *kaṇḍa* 'backbone', rebus: *kaṇḍa* 'stone (ore) metal'.

Back-bone of a seated person shown on a potsherd of the civilization, somewhere on the Sarasati river basin.

I prefer the alternative reading *kaśēru* 'the backbone' (Bengali. Sanskrit); *kaśēruka* id. (Sanskri), rebus: *kasērā* metal worker ' (Lahnda) Lahnda is the name for a dialect of Punjabi close to Bhatinda, an unexcavated site of the civilization on the banks of River Sarasvati. I am confident that the Jury will agree with my hypothesis that the back-bone actually refers to *kasērā* metal worker ' in Meluhha. coppersmith ', Oriya *kā̃sārī,* Hindi *kasārī* m. maker of brass pots'; Gujarati *kā̃sārɔ, kas* m. Maybe, I am prejudging the issue because of Sagan's and my profession as brass-workers. Cognate words are: Assames kā̃hār worker in bell — metal'; Bengali kā̃sāri pewterer, brazier, coppersmith'; Marathi *kā̃sār, kā̃s* m. worker in white metal', *kā̃sārḍā* m. contemptuous term for the same '.Maybe, I prefer this reading because we are recognized as experts in the special quality brass pots which we export to many international destinations to meet the demand of believers in tradition who want

to celebrate the memories of brass work including the use of *jast, satthiya* zinc which had attained international fame after Adolf Hitler abused the svastika glyph. The trial to be decided by Judge Sarsuti is actually a judgement which should indict

Adolf Hitler for the atrocities he committed against business people and metal workers, in general, and against brass-workers, in particular. I think this is an international conspiracy to defame Sagan Muṇḍacaused by the jealousy of the secret recipe Sagan and I use in making the special type of brass which facilitates the preparation of raised script, in bas-relief. I do not have to argue about the rebus reading of the dotted oval.'

Karmi was perhaps referring to another cast tablet excavated from Harappa in 2005 showing an oval glyph ligatured with a short, sloping stroke, flanking the back-bone glyph.

Circular worker platforms discovered in Harappa and Padri.

Two identical glyphs which flank the 'backbone' glyph on these tablets is an oval (variant 'rhombus') sign — like a metal ingot — and is ligatured with an infixed sloping stroke: *ḍhāḷiyum* adj. sloping, inclining (Gujarati)

The ligatured glyph is read rebus as: *ḍhālako* a large metal ingot (Gujarati) *ḍhālakī* a metal heated and poured into a mould; a solid piece of metal; an ingot (Gujarati). Glyph of 'pairing': dula 'pair' (Kashmiri); dul 'cast (metal)' (Santali). A pair of ḍhālako shown on the seal impression on a pot (Mohenjodaro. Text 2937) may connote *dul ḍhālako* 'cast metal ingot'.

So, now we know the function served by the cast metal tablet containing three Indus script glyphs. The artisans were recording and handing over to the scribe of the central accounts office, using the tablet as a record, the cast ingots of brass produed by brass workers working on the circular platforms. The tablets were like bullae which facilitated consolidated accounting and further creation of seals for transporting the consignment of ingots. Then, the inscriptions on seals functioned as bills of lading on the boats which our ancestors used to navigate across the Straits of Hormuz, now called Persian Gulf, crossing Magan and Dilmun to reach Susa. Yes, the same Susa which has yielded the ritual basin and the pot with fish glyph containing metal tools and weapons.

Karmi continued, 'The TV recording studio is a better forum than the courtoom because I am able to show to the viewers the originals of tablets and seals containing Indus script inscriptions. This is also the reason why it is a good idea to make this narrative into a Schindler's List type movie with a cast of actors spanning a period of time from 7th millennium BCE when the first circular hut was made in Bhirrana by Vedic people. It is enough for me to establish in the next follow-up international symposium of Ancient Near East and South Asia-Southeast Asia history experts that the back-bone glyph was the trademark used in hieroglyphs to define a brass-worker professional. The cache of raised-script tablet with identical inscriptions were found in Harappa from a newly-discovered worker platform. Sagan will tell you that our uncle and aunt who live in Padri, Gujarat also worked on a similarly-shaped worker platform within their house. Do you know what was kept in the center of the circular platform? The anvil which produces sparks. Remember, you wanted to know if you were a spark from such an ancient anvil. If you dig deeper into the center of the worker platforms, you are sure to find brass particles chipped off from brass plates while our

ancestor artisans worked on the anvil to shape the plates into pots or other vessels. Now I will recite an ancient song from Rigveda.'

Karmi Hatu took the *śankha* which she had brought from her puja room and blew into it, producing a sound OM which reverberated in the recording hall of ABC News. The News reader was thrilled that the sound of OM would be heard on the live ABC show, heard all over the world and recorded for posterity. Such a sounding of the *śankha* was not permitted in the courtroom of Judge Sarsuti, for reasons of court decorum and judicial propriety. If I had tried that the Prosecutor would have demanded citing me for contempt of court. How can the sound of OM be contempt of court.

Times have changed and memories of people are becoming shorter and shorter.

'This is Vāk,' Karmi said, 'the sacred Word.'

Chapter 19 Karmi sings Nāsadīya sūkta

Karmi Hatu sings the sūkta in the special recording studio of ABC News It is music of the type which ABC News listeners are experiencing for the first time in their lives.

I could not sing the Nāsadīya sūkta in the Courtoom of Judge Sarsuti. Karmi is a brilliant defense counsel. She should have argued in Judge Sarsusti's court.

I should sit with her and take lessons from her. The song is a recitation from Nāsadīya sūkta, the Hymn of Creation from Rigveda, 10.129.

Just imagine the stunning count – from non-existent, from zero to infinity. Only mathematical geniuses should have provided an equation for this metaphor of reckoning. It was a reckoning much beyond Lachesis reckoning the length of the thread from a spindle of one's life.

The *triṣṭup chandas*, a Vedic meter continues: *ná ásat āsīt ná sát āsīt tadânīm* which means 'not the non-existent existed, nor did the existent exist then.'

ná ásat means 'not the non-existent'. The use of the double-negative is as baffling as the word *pūrṇam* in *īśāvāsya upaniṣad,* which refers to the Universe as Infinity and Brahman also as Infinity.

A semantic rhyme occurs in the line: *ná mṛtyúḥ āsīt amŕtam ná tárhi* which means 'then not death existed, nor the immortal.'

An explanation has already been provided in the line: *ânīt avātám svadháyā tát ékam* which means 'breathng without breath, of its own nature, that one.' The process is elaborated like the metallurgical process of alloying copper and zinc in the heat of the furnace: *tápasaḥ tát mahinâ ajāyata ékam* which means 'from contemplation was born that one.'

Who sang this first? The kavayas, pot-seekers They 'found the bond of being within non-being with their heart's thought.'

Is this an elucidation of the process from non-being to being, an enactment of creation?

Here it is in the original text of the song:

Karmi explained the purpose of the sūkta in seven ṛks.

Both this sūkta and the metaphor of Śiva-Naṭarāja's cosmic dance are a description of order which is brought out of chaos; hence, relevant for the discovery of Sarasvati, Vāk, the Divinity, Word.

The birth, disappearance and re-birth of River Sarasvati is a process of bringing order out of chaos.

The song is about creation in the first yajña performed by the the Creator Prajāpati who is the Rṣi who sang this song first.

The song is addressed to Brahman undeveloped in its effects.

1. Then was neither non-existence nor existence: There was no realm of air, no sky beyond it. what covered it, and where? And what gave shelter? Was there, an unfathomed depth of water?
2. Death was not then, nor was there anything immortal: no sign was there, the Day's and Night's divider. That One Thing, breathless, breathed by its own nature: apart from it was nothing whatsoever.
3. Darkness there was: at first concealed in darkness this All was indiscriminated chaos. All that existed then was void and formless: by the great power of Warmth was born that One.

4. Thereafter rose Desire in the beginning, Desire, the primal seed and germ of Spirit. Sages who searched with their heart's thought discovered the kinship of existence with non-existence.
5. Transversely [across the universe] was their dividing line extended: what was above it then, and what below it? There were begetters, there were mighty forces, free action here and energy up yonder.
6. Who verily knows and who can here declare it, whence it was born and whence comes this creation? The Gods are later than this world's production. Who knows then whence it first came into being?
7. He the first origin of this creation, whether he formed it all or did not form it, whose eye controls this world in highest heaven, he verily knows it, or perhaps he knows it not.

Source: Ralph T.H. Griffith, *The Hymns of the Rg Veda*, 1896.

Karmi asked, lifting up her left hand, palm pointing skyward, the way Meluhha merchant greeted the Akkadian buyer: 'Did you hear the words? He surely knows, or maybe He does not! Do you get the message? There cannot be any dogma in a scientific mind. Of course, spiritual quest should coexist with science enquiry, like the satellite imagery analysts in Jodhpur, close to the Vedic Research Foundation, pouring into the series of images transmitted by the IRS 1-C satellite of Indian Space Research Organization and deliberated in a series of international symposia participated in by many experts from all parts of the world.

Karmi continued with the explanation to the TV audience: 'How could breath breathe breathlessly? Obviously, this breath contemplated and desired to create and creation occurred. How was it formed or was it formed at all? Maybe He knows. He is like the sound of the *śankha*.'

So saying, Karmi surprised the ABC News reader. She took the *śankha* conch shell trumpet from her wallet, and blew into it breathlessly with one push of her entire being, her life-force.

The *śankha* released the sound OM which filled the TV recording studio and got transmitted on the satellite channels to all nooks and corners of the world, with millions of viewers left in a state of utter thrall, a state of trance, perhaps a state of siddhi.

For everyone, nothing else mattered but the OM sound emanating from Karmi Hatu's *śankha* conch shell trumpet.

Nothing mattered ! It was all about matter, this *soma* processed on the banks of River Sarasvati, while my ancestors were busy alloying copper with zinc to make shining brass pots, as though they were made of *ancu amśu*, electrum from Mount Mujavata on Pamir plateau of Himalayan chain of mountains stretching from Teheran to Hanoi.' Karmi's voice choked with emotion.

Karmi's hands quivered as she reached out to the cup of tea on the News reader's desk.

Catherine, the News reader was also overcome with emotion. She cleared her throat to announce, 'Thank you, Karmi Hatu. It has been a privilege hearing your breathtaking song. Come back again to enchant our TV viewers around the globe.'

Catherine pressed the button to announce a commercial break for an advertisement announcing a sale of I-pad tablets showing the copper ingot Indus script tablet showing a brass-worker glyph. Brass-worker glyph has become a logo to promote the new patented brand which was creating sales history of unprecedented one million units sold worldwide within the first hour of release.

'I am thankful,' said Karmi, pointing to fish glyph combinations, 'to Michael Korvink for the table showing pairwise combinations and positional order of fish glyphs on inscriptions. Every artistic stroke is meaningful, the same way the strokes on the Daimabad jar showing the rim are meaningful and for which orthographic issue, Sagan has been hauled up in the court of Judge Sarsuti, for a judicial pronouncement. This table of fish glyhph sequences is one example of a falsifiable hypothesis that ligatures on the basic fish glyph were intended to convey a particular 'processed' phase of the metallic mineral during various stages of metalwork – say, from metallic mineral ore phase to metal ingot.'

Chapter 20 Sarasvati, Vāk, speaks

'Sagan finds Sarasvati,' repeated Karmi Hatu.

'Has she spoken?' I asked.

'Yes,' said Karmi, taking a deep breath, as if performing the sacred breathing of *prāṇāyāma*, in a *rājayoga* class.

The tension was becoming unbearable. Judge Sarsuti was waiting for the verdict from the Jury, which had already met in three sessions, in camera. The Judge had laid out, unambiguously, the rules for the Jury deliberations.

What else could I have done to convince the Jury of Sagan's innocence?

Now that Sarasvati has spoken, would it be in violation of the rules of court proceedings to tell the Jury that Sarasvati was a reality, that I should be permitted to present the evidence of her spoken words?

Whatever the rules, it is my dharma to inform the Jury of the new developments which have a clear bearing on the trial. So, I walked into the Judge's chambers and asked for another session in the Court room to inform the Jury on what Sarasvati had spoken.

Judge Sarsuti was most kind. She guided me like a mother to the proprieties of the trial deliberations. She said that she has to consult with the Prosecutor before she could consider telling the Jury about an extension of the trial proceedings.

The Prosecutor said that he has no objection to a limited, time-bound session to hear the words of Sarasvati.

Judge Sarsuti sent a note to the Presiding juror asking for a pause in the Jury deliberations, adding that the Jury can resume after one session to listen to the relayed words of Sarasvati

I was thrilled by the fairness of the justice system while dealing with an unprecedented trial, which had clearly broken new legal grounds to redefine the doctrine of laches dealing with almost infinite time – time almost as divine as Sarasvati herself. It is as though the flow of time itself has been paused for a duration which is infinitesimal compared to the time-infinity that Sarasvati represents. Will Lachesis be recording the moments of my life defending Sagan Muṇḍa?

The Court room session began after a flurry of debates in the media and on talk-shows of ABC News, in particular, about the bizarre turn the trial has taken. Investigative journalists were present in impressive numbers as I started my presentation to the Jury.

'Brothers and sisters,' I addressed the Jury in a confident tone, 'it is a rare privilege that I have been the chosen instrument to relay Sarasvati's words.'

There was pin-drop silence in the Court room, as I paused allowing the historicity of the moment to sink into the hearts and minds of all those present in the Court room.

I continued, 'Sarasvati speaks breaking into chandas छन्दः. Chandas means a Vedic meter. In Hymn 125 of Mandala 10 of Rigveda, the chandas is '

Sarasvati, Vāk has penetrated earth and heaven, holding together all existence.

अहं रुद्रेभिर्वसुभिश्चराम्यहमादित्यैरुतविश्वदेवैः |
अहं मित्रावरुणोभा बिभर्म्यहमिन्द्राग्नीहमश्विनोभा ||

अहं सोममाहनसं बिभर्म्यहं तवष्टारमुतपूषणं भगम |
अहं दधामि दरविणं हविष्मतेसुप्राव्ये यजमानाय सुन्वते ||
अहं राष्ट्री संगमनी वसूनां चिकितुषी परथमायज्ञियानाम |
तां मा देवा वयदधुः पुरुत्राभूरिस्थात्रां भूर्यावेशयन्तीम ||
मया सो अन्नमत्ति यो विपश्यति यः पराणिति य ईंश्र्णोत्युक्तम |
अमन्तवो मां त उप कषियन्ति शरुधिश्रुत शरद्धिवं ते वदामि ||
अहमेव सवयमिदं वदामि जुष्टं देवेभिरुतमानुषेभिः |
यं कामये तं-तमुग्रं कर्णोमि तम्ब्रह्माणं तं रषिं तं सुमेधाम ||
अहं रुद्राय धनुरा तनोमि बरह्मद्विषे शरवे हन्तवा ु |
अहं जनाय समदं कर्णोम्यहं दयावाप्थिवी आविवेश ||
अहं सुवे पितरमस्य मूर्धन मम योनिरप्स्वन्तः समुद्रे |
ततो वि तिष्ठे भुवनानु विश्वोतामूं दयांवर्ष्मणोप सप्रशामि ||
अहमेव वात इव पर वाम्यारभमाणा भुवनानि विश्वा |
परो दिवा पर एना पर्थिव्यैतावती महिना सं बभूव ||

10.125.01a aháṃ rudrébhir vásubhiś carāmi
10.125.01b ahám ādityaír utá viśvádevaiḥ
10.125.01c ahám mitrāváruṇobhā bibharmi
10.125.01d ahám indrāgnī ahám aśvínobha

10.125.02a aháṃ sómam āhanásam bibharmi
10.125.02b aháṃ tváṣṭāram utá pūṣáṇam bhágam
10.125.02c aháṃ dadhāmi dráviṇaṃ havíṣmate
10.125.02d suprāvíye yájamānāya sunvaté

10.125.03a aháṃ rāṣṭrī saṃgámanī vásūnāṃ
10.125.03b cikitúṣī prathamā yajñíyānām
10.125.03c tām mā devā ví adadhuḥ purutrā
10.125.03d bhūriṣṭhātrām bhūri āveśáyantīm

10.125.04a máyā só ánnam atti yó vipáśyati
10.125.04b yáḥ prāṇiti yá īṃ śṛṇóti uktám
10.125.04c amantávo māṃ tá úpa kṣiyanti
10.125.04d śrudhí śruta śraddhiváṃ te vadāmi

10.125.05a ahám evá svayám idáṃ vadāmi
10.125.05b júṣṭaṃ devébhir utá mānuṣebhiḥ
10.125.05c yáṃ kāmáye táṃ-tam ugráṃ kṛṇomi
10.125.05d tám brahmāṇaṃ tám ṛ́ṣiṃ táṃ sumedhām

10.125.06a aháṃ rudrāya dhánur ā tanomi
10.125.06b brahmadvíṣe śárave hántavā u
10.125.06c aháṃ jánāya samádaṃ kṛṇomi
10.125.06d aháṃ dyāvāpṛthivī ā viveśa

10.125.07a aháṃ suve pitáram asya mūrdhán
10.125.07b máma yónir apsú antáḥ samudré
10.125.07c táto ví tiṣṭhe bhúvanānu víśvā
10.125.07d utāmūṃ dyāṃ varṣmáṇópa spṛśāmi

10.125.08a ahám evá vāta iva prá vami
10.125.08b ārábhamāṇā bhúvanāni víśvā
10.125.08c paró divā pará enā pṛthivyā
10.125.08d etāvatī mahinā sám babhūva

'Let me present the song in translation:

<u>Verse I:</u>

Om ! I move along with the Rudras, Vasus, Adithas and all other Devas. I bear the Mithra, Varuna, Indra, Agni and the two Ashwini Devas.

Verse II:

I bear the Soman who is the destroyer of enemies and the Twashta, Pushan and Baga. I give wealth to the performer of the Yajna or Sacrifice who submits sacrificial things in the Yajna, who pours the Soma rasa, and who makes the Devas receive the Havis or their due of the Sacrifice.

Verse III:

I am the Queen of the Universe; I give wealth to those who worship me. I am the all-knowing one and the prime one among the worshippable deities. I enter many bodies as the Atma, taking various forms and with different manifestations, in various ways. Hence, the Devas have incorporated me in various places.

Verse IV:

That one who eats food, who sees, breathes, and hears whatever is said, he does all that only through me (my powers). Those who do not understand me, die. O dear one ! (to the worshipper or devotee), hear this singing of mine with concentration.

Verse V:

"All these are me (and various manifestations of mine). I am the one worshipped by the Devas and the earthly beings. If I like someone (for his meditation towards me), I make him the greatest, the most intelligent as a Sage, and as a Self-Realised soul.

Verse VI:

I bend the bow of the Rudra to kill all those enemies who detest all good things. I fight these bad elements / enemies only for the people. I enter, pervade and persist throughout the earth and the sky.

Verse VII:

I created the sky, which is (as a shelter) above the earth and which is fatherly for all beings. My creativity (power) is within the Ocean and waters. By that, I am present in all the worlds. And I touch the sky with my body.

Verse VIII:

When I start creating all the worlds, I function like the air (so fast in the function). I am taller and higher than the Sky. I am greater than this earth. Such is my valor, might, prowess and greatness."

‘These eight verses, brothers and sisters, are spoken by Vāk. Vāk means ‘speech’. I present my case.’

The Prosecutor raised a point of order. ‘These words are not spoken by Sarasvati, Honorable Judge Sarsuti and Revered Members of the Jury. The words are spoken by Vāk.’

I responded, promptly, ‘The tradition has it that Vāk is Sarasvati. As long as humanity exists, speech exists.’

‘The session ends,’ declared the Judge,. ‘The Jury may adjourn and return with their decision.’

Chapter 21 Karmi takes the case to the viewers of ABC News channel

'The word is divine. The word defines all our existence. Hence, Vāk, is the supreme divinity.' Karmi Hatu paused, gesturing with palms folded in a posture of traditional *namaste*.

' We are dealing with two Juries here. One is in the Courtroom. The other is a composite body of millions of viewers of ABC News Channel and other affiliated TV channels, media outlets the world over. We have listened to Vāk of indeterminate time. As River Sarasvati she nurtured her children on the banks of the rivef flowing in determinate space,' Karmi began the presentation of her defense of Sagan to the TV viewers of a talk-show, 'Her words ring melodious and true. Hers is authentic voice preserved with fidelity, over millennia, almost like a studio Hi-Fi recording, without losing a syllable and without losing a *svara*, or a musical note. Yes, the same way, Sagan prepared the rim of the jar of Daimabad seal, presented in the Indus script corpora. The main issue being deliberated by the Jury is the authenticity of this transcription of the rim of the jar, which is the only glyph on the circular Daimabad seal which has been provenanced as an Indus writing system continuum into the banks of River Pravara, a tributary river of River Godavari, south of the Vindhya mountain ranges. The authenticity of the Daimabad seal inscription is beyond any reasonable doubt. Sagan has been subjected to a heart-breaking trial which has lasted for so long that he and I have lost contact with customers who cherish our Jagadhri brass pots and other brass artifacts. Viewers may be surprised to know that there is a river called Kaveri which runs close to River Pravara and joins the Arabian Sea, flowing westwards, while the other Kaveri flows east and has on her banks, Swamimalai, where metalsmiths of Viśwakarma tradition make Naṭaraja and other exquisite *utsava bera* bronzes, using the *cire perdue* technique of bronze-sculpture-casting, of our ancestor artisans. You have seen how archaeologists have described one of our workshop complexes in Chanhudaro as Sheffield of Ancient India.' Karmi was beaming with pride in relating her facets of her favorite theme of Ancient Indian civilization.

'Tell our viewers about the rim of jar which is the key evidence being debated in the ongoing trial,' intervened the TV talk-show anchor, Catherine, gently directing Karmi Hatu to the main talking point of the trial.

'Thanks, Catherine for bringing me back to reality of the times. Here is an image of the rim of jar dug from Daimabad. The image is the crucial piece of evidence which will exonerate Sagan from the framed-up charge of forgery. Thanks to Reflectance Transformation Imaging (RTI) Technology, the defense counsel was able to conclusively prove to the Jury of the Court that the Daimabad seal, IN FACT, showed rim of jar and not some nondescript doodle.' Karmi displayed the image of the seal and a surface shape sample derived from RTI deployed on an Egyptian hieroglyph Sennedjem Lintel from the Phoebe A. Hearst Museum of Anthropology at the University of California, Berkeley. The RTI blurb reads: “Multiple photographs are taken of an object while light is projected from different angles This lighting information is mathematically synthesized so that examiners can use a computer to analyze, “re-light,” and mathematically enhance the representation of the object’s surface.”

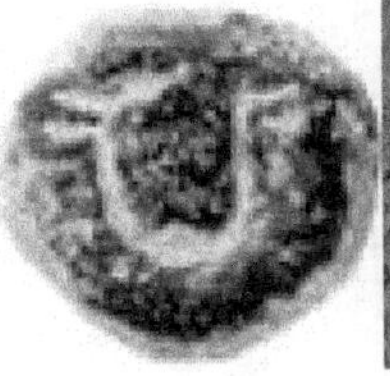

Karmi continued her explanation. 'The curvature of the jar at the mouth got obliterated with the debris and the short stroke on the right-handle of the jar was disfigured to look almost like an apostrophe. The surface shape and angle of the shape of the stroke clearly indicated that the artisan was making an effort to depict the rim of a jar, with a narrow neck. This detail is crucial to demonstrate that the word which should be evoked by any viewer of the image is that of *kanka*.'

This word *kanka* is as significant as Vāk herself. If Vāk signified, *kanka* signified the importance of strokes in an invented writing system which meant a leap in literacy competence of the artisans of yore. Our ancestors had invented what could possibly be the earliest writing system on the globe to denote words with meaning. *Kanka* evoked multiple meanings, the most significant of which was that it meant 'accounting' – by a scribe. Accounting was an organized advancement over the earlier use of tallies and bullae. In Kota language, *kank* means 'calculation, records (government), historical account.'

The accounting process was demonstrated by Karmi Hatu using recent archaeological finds from Harappa by the Harvard Archaeology Project (HARP) of a set of tablets together with a related inscription on a seal. In this instance, the tablets clearly served the purpose of tallies and bullae to keep count on the workers' contribution of artifacts to the guild inventory which had to be couriered to the neighboring Mesopotamian civilization. The inventory had to be unambiguous and provide information required for a bill of materials, including a note on the technology, metallic and non-metallic mineral substances used to produce the artifacts.

Here was the evidence set of tablets and seal shown to the ABC TV channel viewers.

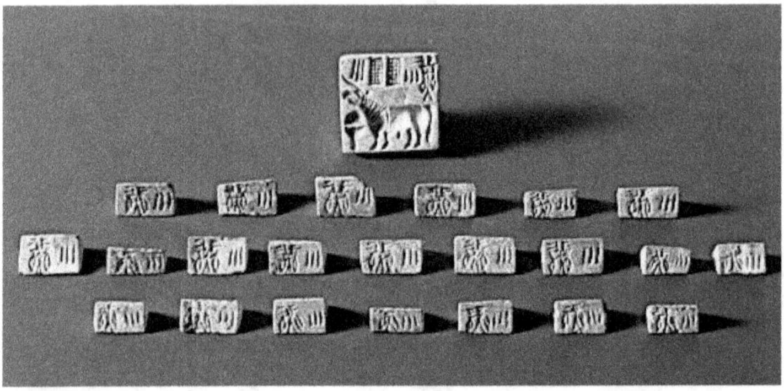

Same inscription, with two glyphs each, was found on twenty-two baked, incised steatite tablets. This inscription become a segment of the message on a seal with a 5-glyph inscription, together a field symbol of a one-horned young bull plus standard device glyphs. The two-glyph inscription conveyed by a set of tablets thus gets semantically expanded into a composite message conveyed through the more elaborately carved seal with a set of 7 glyphs.

So, what was the message? A falsifiable hypothesis can be proposed. The tablets indicated identical artifacts produced on workers' platforms and brought to the scribe, the seal-inscriber, to account for the complete production set of the guild. The tablets were discarded once they had served their purpose as tallies and bullae. The seal which may later be used to create a sealed impression on a package is what becomes important to complete the bill of materials to accompany the courier package.

Let us analyse the components of the inscription on the seal. There are two messages in the two components:

Reading the glyphs on the top register from right to left, we are surprised to find that rim of jar glyph is ligatured to a water-carrier glyph. This glyph is followed by three linear strokes. The water-carrier glyph and the three linear strokes glyph can be read together as *kuti kanka kolme* 'furnace account smithy-forge'. That is, the 22 workers' who delivered tallies (tablets) containing an inscription of the same two glyphs had delivered output from the furnace to the smithy-forge.

The set of glyphs following *kuṭi kanka kolmo* literally meaning 'water-carrier, rim-of-jar, three'; read rebus to mean, 'furnace, account, smithy-forge' are also decoded.

A pair of rectangles with divisions plus three linear strokes denote: *dula khaṇḍ kolmo* literal meaning: 'pair of divisions, three'; read rebus. The pair of rectangles with divisions can be read as *dul kaṇḍ*, meaning 'cast (ingot) metal.' In Santali language of our ancestors, *dula* means 'pair'; rebus: *dul* means 'cast (metal)(Santali). Together with the three linear strokes (kolmo), the rebus reading of the message in this component is: *dul kaṇḍ kolami* 'cast (metal) ingot to smithy-forge'.

It is clear that there are two sets of workers performing two sets of functions. The first function is production of metal from the furnace. The second function is casting of metal in smithy-forge.

Thus, it may be proposed that the two-part inscription on the seal denoted two messages: 1. Output from furnace accounted to smithy-forge; 2. Cast (ingot) metal accounted to smithy-forge. The smithy-forge is the common recipient connoted by the glyph of three linear strokes. *kolmo* means 'three'; rebus: *kolami* 'smithy-forge'.

The glyphs of one-horned young bull calf and the standard device can also be read rebus: *kũdār* 'turner' *koḍ* 'workshop'; *sangaḍa* 'gimlet, portable furnace'; rebus: *jangāḍiyo* 'military guard to accompany the treasure'.

Thus, the entire inscribed message on the seal indicates that the furnace output and cast (metal) ingot to smithy-forge (*kolami*) are ready (worked on smithy-forge), packaged to be couriered by *kũdār koḍ jangāḍiyo* , that is, 'turner-workshop treasure-guard'. Creating a sealed impression using the seal will complete the bill of lading information on the sealed package. Several such packages can be pooled together – as a composite shipment -- by stringing together the related seals used to create sealed impressions on respective packages.

saghaḍī = furnace (G.)
san:ghaṭi = a millstone, that crushes (Ka.)

The accounting for the consignment is complete; the consignment is ready to be shipped.

We know that water-carrier glyph is read rebus *kuṭi* 'furnace'. Thus, *kuṭi* 'furnace' plus *kanka* 'rim of jar' indicate that the products which came from 22 tablets of 22 workers' platforms were part of 'furnace accounting' system. More specifically, the rim of jar was *kaṇḍ kanka*. The word *kand* 'pot' is relatable to *kaṇḍ* 'metallic mineral' as in *ayaskaṇḍa* 'excellent quantity of metal'. *kaṇḍ* in Santali means 'altar, furnace'; thus the word can be more precisely explained as 'metallic mineral subjected to smelting in a furnace' – to be distinguished from, say, a stone of meteoric iron. The glyphs of one-horned bull calf and standard device were indicative of the guild of turner-workshop. *kolmo* means 'three'. That *kolmo* is the word is denoted by three linear strokes. *kolmo* read rebus refers to *kolami* 'forge, smithy'. From the furnace to the forge, the processing and accounting process is complete.

The significance of the strokes depicting rim of jar reinforce the innocence of Sagan who should be a free man and discharged by the Court from the false allegation of claim of forgery of the glyph on Daimabad seal.

'How lucky!' exclaimed Karmi, 'these people working for HARP have the *anugraham* of Devi Vāk that they are not only able to find out the accounting process from furnace to forge, smithy but also to provide an archaeologically-falsifiable positing of two distinct functions of metal-wokers to decipher the words and the writing system to explain the two specific functions in metal-work.'

Karmi went on to narrate the discovery of the 'water-carrier' hieroglyph – not on any site on the banks of River Sarasvati, but beyond the navigable Persian Gulf, in Ur, on the right bank of River Euphrates. The sea-faring merchants of Meluhha had navigated the River Sarasvati, Persian Gulf and Rivers Tigris and Euphrates for exchange of commodities. All the wealth which got exchanged with Mesopotamia from the sea route, had to pass through Ur. Hebrew patriarch Abram was born in Ur. He was also called Abraham or Oraham in Aramaic or Ibrahim in Arabic.

The Ziggurat of Ur had the shrine of Nanna, the moon divinity. There were Meluhha settlements in Sumer and Mesopotamia.

The water-carrier glyph is flanked on either side by a pair of star glyphs. *meḍha* 'polar star' is rebus for *meḍ* 'iron'. Thus the reading of the composite of glyphs is *meḍ kuṭi* 'iron furnace'.

Bahrain seal: four antelope heads emanating from a star. *meḍha* 'polar star'

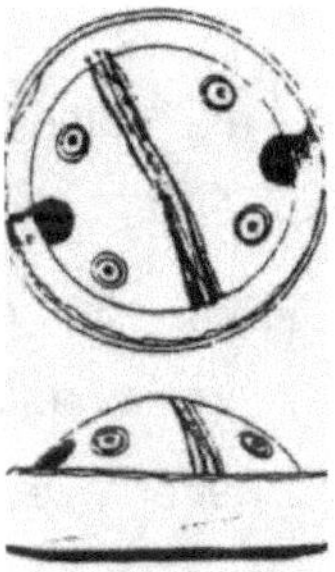

(Marathi). *meḍ* 'iron' (Ho.Mu.) Allograph: meḍh 'ram'. Rebus: *meṛh* 'helper of merchant'.

A tree is shown on this Dilmun seal.

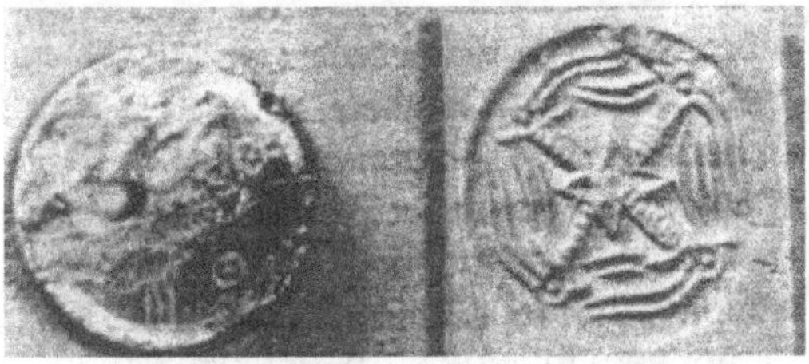

Glyph: 'tree': khuṭi 'tree'. Rebus: kuṭhi 'smelter furnace' (Santali).

Evidence of long distance relations in the early second millennium BCE is seen on a Dilmun seal from Barbar; six heads of antelope radiating from a circle; similar to animal protomes in Failaka, Anatolia and Indus.

Glyph: 'ladder': H. *sainī, senī* f. ladder ' Rebus: Pa. *sēṇi* -- f. guild, division of army '; Pk. *sēṇi* -- f. row, collection '; śrḗṇi (metr. often *śrayaṇi* --) f. line, row, troop ' RV. The lexeme in Tamil means: Limit, boundary; எல்லை. நளியிரு முந்நீரேணி யாக (புறநா. 35, 1). Country, territory.

The glyphics are repeated on a circular seal of Mohenjo-daro. It shows a warrior. Mohenjo-daro seal m417 six heads from a core.

Semantics: 'group of animals/quadrupeds': paśu 'animal' (RV), *pasaramu, pasalamu* = an animal, a beast, a brute, quadruped (Te.) Rebus: *pasra* 'smithy' (Santali)

> *paśú* m., *páśu* -- n. domestic or sacrificial animal ' RV. m. goat ' lex. Pa. *pasu* -- , *°uka* -- m. cattle '; Aś.shah. man. *paśu* -- , gir. kāl. dh. jau. *pasu* -- beast ', NiDoc. *paśu*, Pk. *pasu*<-> m. animal, horned quadruped, goat, sheep ', Ap. *pasuva* -- m.; Kt. *paċə -- moč* shepherd '; S. *paha* f. goat '; A. *pâha* animal of the deer class, any quadruped '; H. *pas* f. buffalo -- heifer ', *pasū̃* m. animal (such as goat or sheep) '. *paśú* -- : S.kcch. *paū̃* f. she -- goat '; WPah.poet. *pɔśu* m. cattle, head of cattle, animal ' (Him.I 117 ← H.). (CDIAL 7984).

Glyph: 'six': *bhaṭa* 'six'. Rebus: *bhaṭa* 'furnace'.

Glyph (the only inscription on the Mohenjo-daro seal m417): 'warrior': *bhaṭa*. Rebus: *bhaṭa* 'furnace'. Thus, this glyph is a semantic determinant of the message: 'furnace'. It appears that the six heads of 'animal' glyphs are related to 'furnace' work. The depiction of glyph: 'tree' is indicative that the entire composition is also related to 'smelter' work: *khuṭi* tree'. Rebus: *kuṭhi* 'smelter furnace' (Santali).

These are joined animals. The lexeme *sangaḍa* 'joined animals'. Rebus: *sangāta* 'association, guild'. *jangāḍiyo*, 'military guard accompanying treasure.'

1. Glyph: 'one-horned heifer': *kondh* 'heifer'. *kũdār* 'turner, brass-worker'.

2. Glyph: 'bull': *ḍhangra* bull'. Rebus: *ḍhangar* blacksmith'.

3. Glyph: 'ram': *meḍh* 'ram'. Rebus: *meḍ* 'iron' Rebus: *meṛh* 'helper of

merchant'.

4. Glyph: 'antelope': *mreka* 'goat'. Rebus: *milakkhu* 'copper'. Vikalpa 1: *meluhha* ' *mlecchā* 'copper worker'.

5. Glyph: 'zebu': *khū̃ṭ* 'zebu'. Rebus: *khū̃ṭ* 'guild, community' (Semantic determinant of the 'jointed animals' glyphic composition). *kūṭa* joining, connexion, assembly, crowd, fellowship (DEDR 1882) Pa. *gotta* 'clan'; Pk. *gotta, gōya* id. (CDIAL 4279) Semantics of Pkt. lexeme *gōya* is concordant with Hebrew *'goy'* in *ha-goy-im* (lit. the-nation-s)·

6. The sixth animal can only be guessed. Perhaps, a tiger (A reasonable inference, because the glyph 'tiger' appears in a procession on some Indus script inscriptions. Glyph: 'tiger?': *kol* 'tiger'. Rebus: *kol* 'worker in iron'. Vikalpa (alternative): perhaps, rhinoceros. Glyph: *baḍhi* 'castrated boar'. Rebus: *baḍhoe* 'worker in wood and iron'.

Thus, the entire glyphic composition of six animals on the Mohenjodaro seal m417 is semantically a representation of a *śrḗṇi,* 'guild', a *khū̃ṭ,* 'community' of smiths and masons. Cognate with gotta 'clan' (Pali).

Kharoṣṭī goy, Harosheth hagoyim, 'smithy of nations'

Harosheth in Hebrew: םייוגה תשורח is pronounced *khar-o-sheth.*

Ha-ro'-sheth or (charosheth) ha-goyim is a reference to a place name, which occurs in the Bible in the following contexts:

> Judges 4:2 Yahweh sold them into the hand of Jabin king of Canaan, who reigned in Hazor; the captain of whose army was Sisera, who lived in Harosheth of the Gentiles.

Judges 4:13 Sisera gathered together all his chariots, even nine hundred chariots of iron, and all the people who were with him, from Harosheth of the Gentiles, to the river Kishon.

Judges 4:16 But Barak pursued after the chariots, and after the army, to Harosheth of the Gentiles: and all the army of Sisera fell by the edge of the sword; there was not a man left.

The morpheme גּוֹי (*goy*) in hagoyim means a 'nation, gentile' and hence, hagoyim is interpreted as 'of nations'. Maybe, '-goy-' is cognate with Prakrit goy meaning a 'clan'.

Pali. *gotta* -- n. 'clan', Prakrit. *gotta* -- , *gutta* -- , amg. *gōya* -- n.; Gau. *gū* 'house' (in Kaf. and Dard. several other words for cowpen ' > 'house': gōṣṭhá -- , Pr. *gū´ṭu* cow '; S. *goṭru* m. parentage ', L. *got* f. clan ', P. *gotar*, *got* f.; Ku. N. *got* 'family '; A. *got -- nāti* 'relatives '; B. *got* clan '; Or. *gota* family, relative '; Bhoj. H. *got* m. family, clan ', G. *got* n.; M. *got* 'clan, relatives '; -- Si. *gota* 'clan, family ' ← Pa.

The word goya denotes descent from a common ancestor, with a common occupation, like members of a guild. Gotta in Prakrit probably means agnate rather than cognate. There is no word in English for gotta. It includes all those descended, or supposed to be descended, from a common ancestor. In the Torah/Hebrew Bible, goy and its variants appear in reference to Israelites and to Gentile nations. Maybe, aramaean traders spread out into Central Asia and their writing system of Aramaic led to the evolution of another syllabic writing system, kharoṣṭī by Hindu meluhha, mleccha traders passing up the Persian gulf and becoming acquainted with the systems of writing in Mesopotamia and Aramaic alphabet. It may be possible to trade Brahmi and kharoṣṭī glyphs with Aramaic and Hebrew phonographic glyphs.

Coins of Agathocles, satrap of Paropamisade between Bactria and India use the legend 'Basileos Agathokleous' ('of King Agathocles'), 'Rajane Agathuklayasa' in Brahmi, sometimes also in kharoṣṭī. An expert notes, 'Coins with legends in Kharosthi have been found from almost all chronological span of the script, including issues of the Indo-Greeks, Indo-Scythians, Indo-Parmians, Kusanas, Ksatrapas, Audumbaras, Kulutas, Kunindas, Rajanyas, Vemakis and Vṛṣṇis… A few Sino-Kharosthi coins, bearing inscriptions in both Chinese and Kharosthi, have been discovered in and around Hotan.' British Library has a collection of twenty-nine birch bark fragments containing the work of twenty-one different scribes, reportedly found in Hadda, Afganistan.

Coin of Agathocless of Bactria. Possibly minted in Taxila. Railed tree, Kharoṣṭī legend below: hiranasme (golden hermitage) /

Six-arched hill, Kharoṣṭī legend below: akathukreyasa

Bactria: Agathocles, AE dichalkon, c. 185-170 BCE

Weight: 4.90 gm., Dim: 20 x 14 mm., Die axis: 12 h

Greek legend: ΒΑΣΙΛΕΩΣ ΑΓΑΘΟΚΛΕΟΥΣ

Indo-Greek: Apollodotus I, Silver Attic weight hemidrachm, c. 174-165 BCE

Weight: 1.74 gm., Diam: 14 mm., Die axis: 12 h

Elephant walking right, Greek legend around:

ΒΑΣΙΛΕΩΣ ΑΠΟΛΛΟΔΟΤΟΥ ΣΩΤΗΡΟΣ /

Humped bull walking right, Kharoṣṭī legend around:

maharajasa apaladatasa tratarasa

Indo-Greek: Apollodotus I, Silver "Indian" weight drachm, c. 174-165 BCE

Weight: 2.38 gm., Dim: 15 x 16 mm., Die axis: 12 h

Elephant walking right, Greek legend on three sides:

ΒΑΣΙΛΕΩΣ ΑΠΟΛΛΟΔΟΤΟΥ ΣΩΤΗΡΟΣ

monogram below /

Humped bull standing right, Kharoṣṭī legend on three sides:

maharajasa apaladatasa tratarasa

Indo-Greek: Antimachus II, Silver drachm, c. 174-165 BCE

Weight: 2.37 gm., Diam: 16 mm., Die axis: 12 h

Winged Nike standing left, holding wreath and palm, monogram left,

Greek legend around: ΒΑΣΙΛΕΩΣ ΝΙΚΗΦΟΡΟΥ ΑΝΤΙΜΑΧΟΥ /

Horseman galloping right,

Kharoṣṭī legend around: Maharajasa jayadharasa Amtimakhasa

Bactria: Agathocles, AE double karshapana, c. 185-170 BCE

Weight: 14.45 gm., Dim: 22 x 27 mm., Die axis: 12 h

Female deity moving left, holding flower

Brahmi legend: Rajane Agathukleyasasa /

Lion standing right,

Greek legend: ΒΑΣΙΛΕΩΣ
ΑΓΑΘΟΚΛΕΟΥΣ

Bilingual silver drachm of Menander I (160-135 BC). With obverse and reverse legends in Grfeek "BASILEOS SOTĒROS MENANDROY" and Kharoṣṭī "MAHARAJA TRATASA MENADRASA": "Of The Saviour King Menander". Reverse shows Athena advancing right, with thunderbolt and shield.

Indian-standard coin of Apollodotus (180–160 BCE).

Bilingual coin of Eucratides in the Indian standard, on the obverse Greek inscription reads: *ΒΑΣΙΛΕΩΣ ΜΕΓΑΛΟΥ ΕΥΚΡΑΤΙΔΟΥ*- "(of) King Great Eucratides", Pali in the Kharoṣṭī script on the reverse.

Kharoṣṭī and Aramaic, cognate writing systems

Kharoṣṭī code also called Arian Pali traces back to the time of Achaemenid conquest and occupation of Gandhāra region in northwestern India from 559 to 336 BCE. Kharoṣṭī code was most likely used by Kharahostes gotta in continuation of the harosheth hagoyim tradition enshrined in the Bible (*Judges*) which is the tradition of the smithy of nations exemplified by the axle-pin of the war chariot detailed in *Judges*.

The smithy traditions date back to Meluhha code.

The kharoṣṭī signs for a, ca, da, na, ya, ra, va, s'a, sa, za and ha present little difficulty as they can be derived more or less directly from their Aramaic counterparts alep, sadeh, dalet, nun, bet, yod, res, waw, het, samek, zayin and he.

The letters ka, kha, ga, ta and pa do not match the Aramaic letters kap, qop, gimel, taw, and peh, which show a closer resemblance to Kharosthi da, sa, ya, pa and a respectively. Probably each form da, sa, ya, pa and a was created before ka, kha, ga, ta and pa.

Geographical extent of the Kharoṣṭhī script

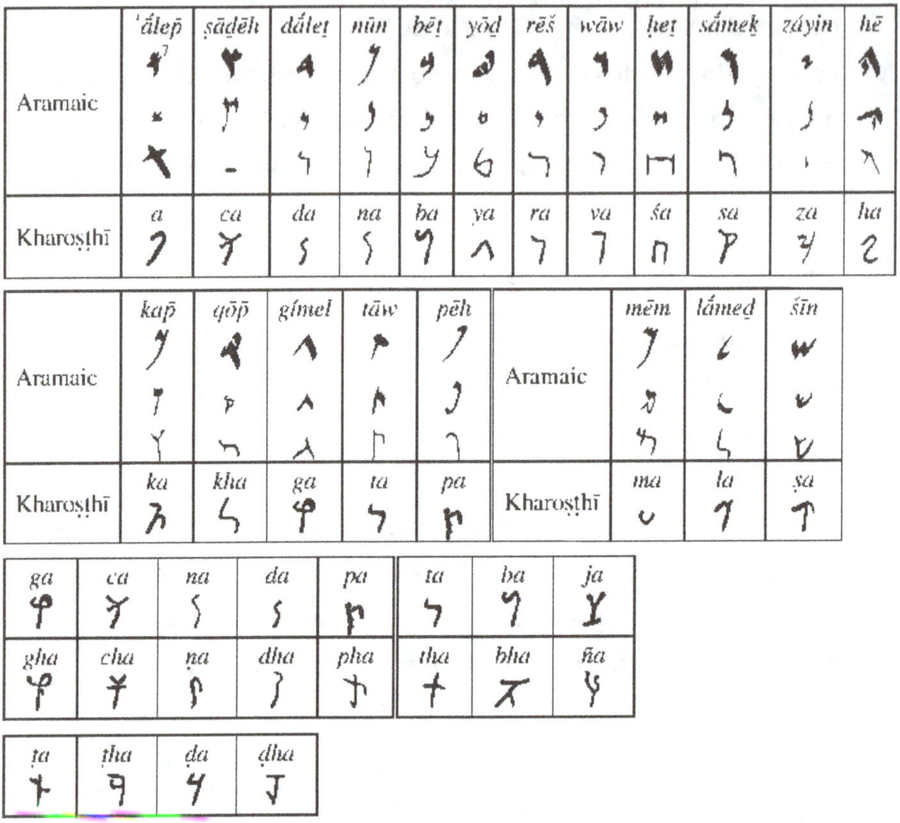
'ālep̄ ṣādēh dālet nūn bēt yōd rēš wāw ḥet sāmek záyin hē
Aramaic
a ca da na ba ya ra va śa sa za ha
Kharoṣṭhī
kap̄ qōp̄ gímel tāw pēh
Aramaic
ka kha ga ta pa
Kharoṣṭhī
mēm lāmed šīn
Aramaic
ma la ṣa
Kharoṣṭhī
ga ca na da pa ta ba ja
gha cha ṇa dha pha tha bha ña
ṭa ṭha ḍa ḍha

What did 'harosheth' signify? I suggest, said Karmi Hatu, that the word is cognate with Prakrit *kharoṣṭī* which is derived from *khara* + *oṣṭa* meaning 'blacksmith + lip'.

This guild, community of smiths and masons evolves into Harosheth Hagoyim, 'a smithy of nations'.

It appears that the Meluhhans were in contact with many interaction areas, Dilmun and Susa (elam) in particular. There is evidence for Meluhhan settlements outside of Meluhha. It is a reasonable inference that the Meluhhans with bronze-age expertise of creating arsenical and bronze alloys and working with other metals constituted the 'smithy of nations', Harosheth Hagoyim.

The lead players identified in the war are General Sisera who was killed by Jael.

A biblical scholar identifies the root verb חרשׁ (*harash*)', meaning ' to engrave or plough'; the noun 'חרשׁת (*haroshet*)', means a 'carving'.

Hence, kharoṣṭī came to represent a 'carving, engraving' art, i.e. a writing system.

Cognae Indo-aryan words are: karṣá m. dragging ' Pāṇ., agriculture ' Āp. [Cf. *kā́rṣi* -- ploughing ' TS., *karṣí* -- Kapiṣṭh.: √kr̥ṣ]
Pk. *karisa* -- m. dragging ', *kassa* -- m. mud '; Paš. *kaṣ* pulling '; Or. *kāsa* time or turn of ploughing a field '. karṣaka cultivating ', m. husbandman ' Yājñ. [karṣá -- : √kr̥ṣ]
Pa. *kassaka* -- m. ploughman ', Pk. *karisaya* -- , *kāsaya* -- , *°sava* -- m.; Si. *kasayā* peasant ', *kasu -- kama* ploughing, agriculture '; -- H. *kassā* m. mattock ', *°sī* small do. ' karṣaṇa n. tugging, ploughing, hurting ' Mn., cultivated land ' MBh. [kárṣati, √kr̥ṣ]
Pk. *karisaṇa* -- n. pulling, ploughing '; G. *karsaṇ* n. cultivation, ploughing '; OG. *karasaṇī* m. cultivator ', G. *karasṇī* m. kárṣati draws, pulls ' RV. [√kr̥ṣ]
Pa. *kassatē* ploughs '; Pk. *karisaï*, *kāsaï* pulls '; Gy. pal. *kšal* -- to drag, pull, lead ', arm. *kaš* -- to pull ' karṣí furrowing ' Kapiṣṭh. [Cf. *kā́rṣi* -- ploughing ' VS., *karṣū́* -- f. furrow, trench ' ŚBr.: √kr̥ṣ]
Pr. *kṣe_* plough -- iron ', Paš. *kaṣí* mattock, hoe '; Shum. *káṣi* spade, pickaxe '; S. *kasī* f. trench, watercourse '; L. *kass* m. catch drain, ravine ', *kassī* f. small distributing channel from a canal '; G. *kās* m. artificial canal for irrigation ' -- Dm. Phal. *khaṣī́* small hoe '

A cognate word is: kr̥ṣṭiḥ कृष्टि: 'drawing, pulling', 'inhabitants', 'teacher', 'men , races of men '. With the word harosheth, we seem to be remembering nations with smithy engraving competence, that is, use of Meluhha code of smithy scribes.

This set of words points to the association of harosheth with metal tools or metalwork – ploughshare, in particular -- leading to the interpretation of harosheth as 'smithy'. The context provided by the Judges of the Bible confirms that at the place called Harosheth hagoyim, iron war chariots were made. Sisera in the Judges called together nine hundred iron chariots.

An exciting archaeological discovery related to an axle of such a war chariot. Rigveda (X.22.11) has a reference to ākṣāṇa, 'axle-pin' composed of roots, akṣa, 'axle' and āṇi, 'pin'.

A 3,200-year-old round bronze tablet with a carved face of a woman, found at the El-ahwat excavation site near Katzir in central Israel, is part of a linchpin that held the wheel of a battle chariot in place. This could be close to Harosheth Hagoyim. The metal pin might have been product of a Meluhhan smithy. The round, bronze tablet, about 2 cm. in diameter and 5 mm. thick, was found in a structure identified as the "Governor's House". The object features a carved face of a woman wearing a cap and earrings shaped as chariot wheels. It was the top broken end of a long axle-linchpin. Use of such linchpins is demonstrated on some Egyptian reliefs.

7" long Philistie bronze linchpin discovered at site of Ashkelon.

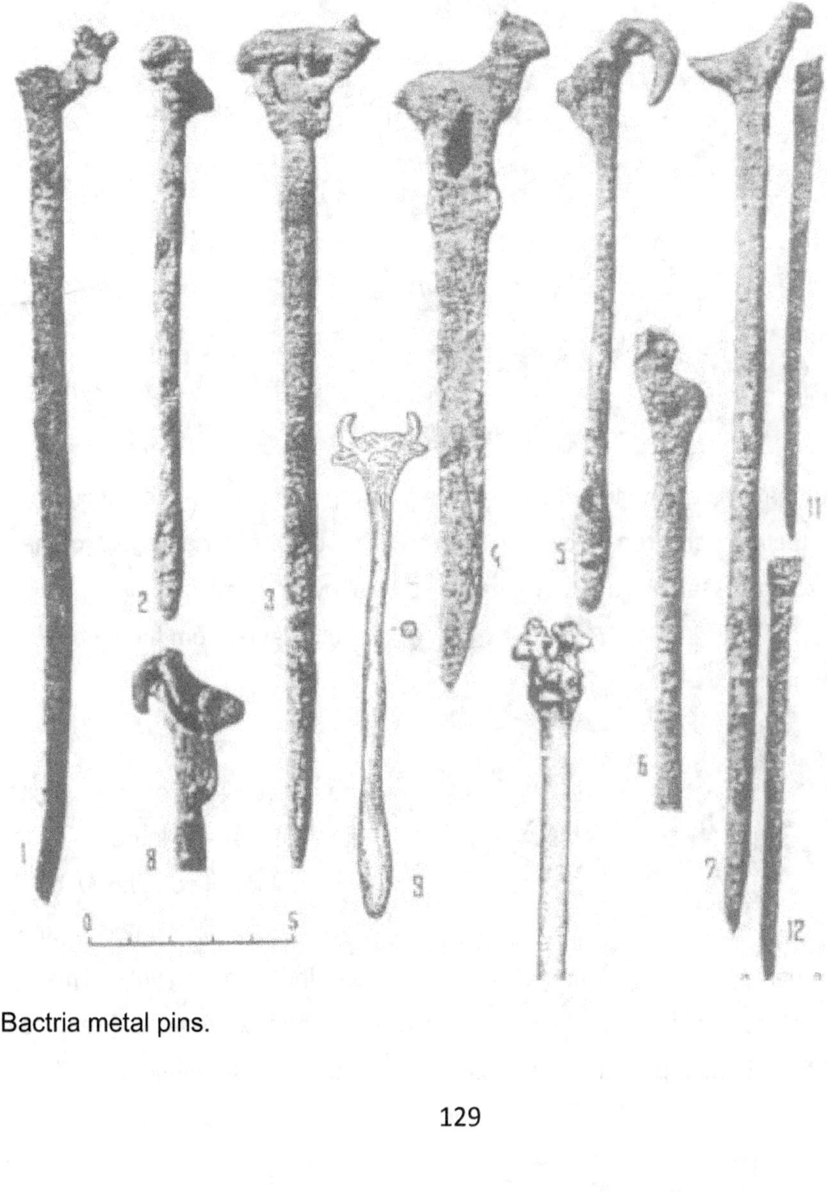

Bactria metal pins.

The facial features on the top of the linchpin is comparable to the face of Hariti, divine protector of children, shown on this rondel made of silver and gold, of the ancient region of Gandhāra. The bronze rondels showing heads are also

comparable, from the same region.

There is a possibility that this seal impression from an Elamite site, Haft Tepe, a large archaeological complex with seven mounds, located 10 kms. south of Susa, had some connections with scribes of Indian hieroglyphs. This requires further investigation. Let me cite from *Encyclopaedia Iranica*: "From Haft Tepe (Middle Elamite period, ca. 13th century) in Ḵūzestān an unusual pyrotechnological installation was associated with a craft workroom containing such materials as mosaics of colored stones framed in bronze, a dismembered elephant skeleton used in manufacture of bone tools, and several hundred bronze arrowpoints and small tools. Situated in a courtyard directly in front of this workroom is a most unusual kiln. This kiln is very large, about 8 m long and 2 and one half m wide, and contains two long compartments with chimneys at

each end, separated by a fuel chamber in the middle. Although the roof of the kiln had collapsed, it is evident from the slight inturning of the walls which remain in situ that it was barrel vaulted like the roofs of the tombs. Each of the two long heating chambers is divided into eight sections by partition walls. The southern heating chamber contained metallic slag, and was apparently used for making bronze objects. The northern

heating chamber contained pieces of broken pottery and other material, and thus was apparently used for baking clay

objects including tablets . . .”

This is the impression of Middle Elamite carnelian cylinder seal in Mittanian style. The vivid glyphs are: a star and mollusk flanked by two antelopes, indicating the Indus words *meḍh* and *hangi*. *meḍh* 'star'; 'ram'. Rebus: *meḍ* 'iron' Rebus: *meṛh* 'helper of merchant'; *hangi* 'mollusc' Rebus: *sanghi* 'priest accompanying caravan; possibly, 'member of guild'.

Susa ritual basin decorated with goatfish figures, molluscs.

The glyphs evoke the tradition of Susa ritual basin on which the antelopes were replaced by 'goat-fish' ligatured glyphs.

Rock relief of Bisutun. The trilingual inscriptions are in Elamite, Babylonian and Old Persian. Overthrown rulers are listed as 1. Gaumāta (in Magia); 2. Āçina (in Elam); 3. Nadintabaira (in Babylon); 4. Martiya (in Elam); 5. Fravartiš (in Media); 6. Čiçantaxma (in Sagartia); 7. Frāda (in Marv); 8. Vahyazdāta (in Arachosia); 9. Araxa (in Babylon).

Greek author Eratosthenes of 3rd century BCE named a nation called Ariane which is derived from an old Iranian phrase, 'āryānām xṣāṭram' which meant 'land of the Aryans'. Bactrians, Chorasmians, Sogdians, Sakas, Persians and Medes claimed themselves to be of common origin and with kinship of the languages they spoke in a region which stretched from the northern coast of Black Sea to the area now called Afghanistan. Bisutun inscription of 518 BCE lists Iranian regions as Margiana, Bactria, other Central Asian states, Gandhāra and Sattagydia in the east. Avesta written in Helmand/Hari-rud valley, refers to Viṣtāspa, patron of Zoroaster who preached in area called *airyānem vaējō*. By mid-first millennium BCE, citadels have been found in settlements of upto 5 hectare area in southwest Turkmenistan. Arrian's Anabasis (VI.24.3) refers to Cyrus' attack on 'the land of the Indians', where the Iranians lost a large part of their forces. Before 600 BCE, they acquired land in Elam entering service of rulers as cavalry. Sakas were also in northern and central Asia and Eastern Turkestan, while Scythians were of Pontic steppes and all spoke ancient versions of Indus language (meluhha, mleccha). Zantupati was the chief who united clan communes who made up a province called dahyu. This word dahyu is also called dasyu in Manu. Zanta, 'commune', literally meant 'peaceful dwellers'. According to an account of Berossus and Ctesias, Cyrus died fighting Dahae, a Scythian people of Middle Asia. Ctesias adds that the last battle of Cyrus was against the Derbices, supported by Indians who used battle elephants. An Indian speared Cyrus and the wound in the liver proved fatal three days later. Manu notes (10.45) the existence of a mleccha-speaking community among dasyu:

mukhabāhuroopajjānām yā loke jātayo bahih

mlecchavācas' cāryavācas te sarve dasyuvah smṛtāh

"All those people of the world which are excluded from the (community of) those born from the mouth, the arms, the thighs and the feet (of Brahman) are called Dasyu, whether they speak the language of the mleccha or that of the Arya." This statement of Manu clearly meant that mleccha dialect speakers and arya dialect speakers are all remembered as dasyu. In Mahabharata, Pahlava, Shabara, Saka, Yavana, Pundra, Kirata, Dramida, Simbhala, Barbara, Darada and Mleccha are collectively summed up as mleccha (1.165.35-37). Mleccha is the ungrammatical *lingua franca* as distinct from grammatically correct, literary bhāṣā which was proto-Sanskrit or chandas in Vedic parlance. Sanskrit (refined speech) is distinguished from asura, pisaca, mleccha as dialects with variant pronunciation of Samskṛtam. For instance, *śatapatha brāhmaṇa* notes that the mleccha-speakers failed to articulate arava(h) correctly; they uttered 'helava helava'. (*te asura attavacasa he'alave he'alava* 3.2.1.23). One notes that the madhyandina-branch of the *ś*atapathi brahmins were occasionally indifferent to correct articulation; so that they got corrupt recitation as the mleccha did.

Ptolemy (VII.1.55) names the region along the course of River Sindhu as Indo-Scythia which included Patalene, Abiria and Surashtra. kharoṣṭī inscriptions of Sakas and coins of Maues (Moga), a Saka and Azes, a Pahlava were found in the Panjab, Swat and Kashmir foothills. Some Maues coins have 'Basileous

Mauou' in Greek ('of King Maues') and equivalent kharoṣṭī on the reverse, *'mahārājasa Moasa'.*

Some coins have 'Basileos Basileon Megalou Mauou' 'of the Great King of Maues' with Prakrit version in kharoṣṭī, *'rājatirājasa mahātasa Moasa'.*

Similar legends were used on coins of Azes:

ΒΑΣΙΛΕΩΣ ΒΑΣΙΛΕΩΝ ΜΕΓΑΛΟΥ ΑΖΟΥ, *rājatirājasa Mahārājasa rājarājasa mahātasa.* Three principal mints were used by Azes I. one at Puṣkalāvati (Gāndhāra), another at Taxila and the third in a middle Sindhu province. Kṣatraps Jihoṇika (Zeionises) and Rājuvūla and *strategoi* (Indian equivalent of *senapati*, 'commander of the army') Indravarma and Aśpavarma also issued coins. '*Xṣacapavan*' is Old Persian word for Kṣatrap meaning 'protector of the realm'.

The inscription on Mathura lion capitol records that a teacher named Budhila was given a gift so that he might teach the Mahāsanghikas. The gift of a stupa with a relic of the Buddha, was given by Queen Ayasia Kamuia, 'wife of Rājuvūla' and 'daughter of Kharahostes'. Kharahostes was an Indo-Scythian ruler in northern Indian subcontinent around 10 BCE to 10 CE. Also recorded is a religious gift of Kṣatrapa śodāsa, son of Rājuvūla, in honour of Mahākṣatrapa Kutuluka Patika and Kṣatrapa Mevaki Miyika in honour of the whole of Sakastan.

Coins of Kharahostes

Obverse: King on horseback, with levelled spear. Greek legend XAPAHWCTEI CATPAΠEI ARTAYOY ("Satrap Kharahostes, son of Arta"). Kharoahthi mint mark *sam* 

Kharahostes' coinage bear a dynastic mark (a circle within three pellets), comparable to the mark of a contemporary ruler, Kujula Kadphises (three pellets joined together).

Reverse: Lion. *kharoṣṭī* legend *Kharahostei satrapei Artauou' : 'Kṣatrapasa Pra Kharaoṣtasa Artasa Putrasa* (Of Satrap Kharaosta, son of Arta). *Kharaoṣta* may be derived *from khara + oṭṭha*, i.e. lit. 'blacksmith' + 'lip'. *Oṭṭha* [Vedic oṣṭha, Avestan. aosta lip; Lat. ōs mouth = Sk. āḥ] the lip (Pali). The name of a writing system, *kharoṣṭī* is similarly derived from khara oṭṭi ‘blacksmith voice’.

‘I will demonstrate,’ said Karmi Hatu with confidence, ‘that the method of writing using hieroglyphs evidences in Susa, Hafta Tepe and Indus script inscriptions

continued into the periods even when *kharoṣṭī* script was in vogue. Two examples can be cited of the use of mollusc hieroglyph read rebus as *sanghi*: one is that of Mathura lion capitol and the other of Sanchi stupa’. The message is the same in both examples: veneration – puja -- of ariya dhamma and

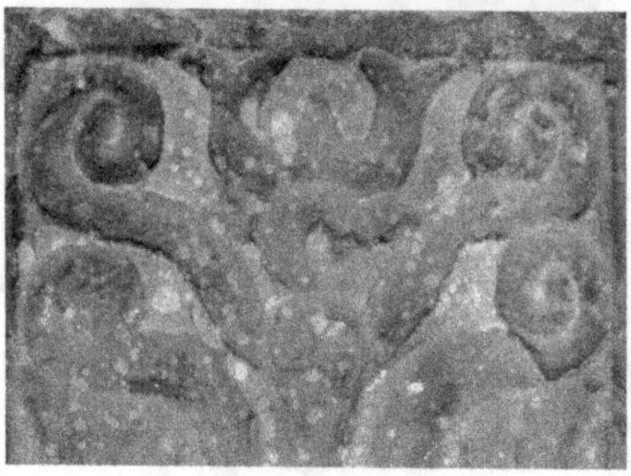

sangha dhamma. Also, the tradition of stupa was a continuum of the ziggurat tradition of venerating ancestors’.

The mollusc glyph is used on Mathura lion capital dated circa 120 BCE, flanked by two recumbent lions. An embellishment added to the mollusk composition is *śrivatsa* glyph of two ligatured fish-tails. The sculpture has an inscription in Prakrit using *kharoṣṭī* script.

The sthapati shown carries a mallet: Glyph: kūṭa, ‘mallet’. Rebus: kūṭa ‘chief (of guild)’. Glyph: *daḷa* þetals (on circle)’. Rebus: *daḷa* ɠuild’. The entire composition is *ayira dhamma sangha daḷa; arya kūṭa* 'Guild-community (practicing) ariya dhamma'.

Sanchi eastern torana architrave.

ayira 'fish'; dhama 'tie'; hangi 'snail'; pair 'dul'; rebus: arya, ayira 'noble'; dhama 'global ethic': ayira dhama; ayira sangha 'community'; dol 'picture, form'. ayira 'fish'; rebus: metath. ayira 'noble'. Together, read: *ariya sangha*. Thus, the composition connotes the message: ariya dhamma, ariya sangha. Ariya is denoted by the pair of seated lions ara 'lion'.

The inscription details donors and donations to Mahasanghikas.

Transcript.

A. I.[2]

1. **Mahachhatravasa Rajulasa**
2. **agramaheshia**[3] **Yasia**
3. **Kamudhaa dhitra**
4. **Kharaostasa yuvaraña**
5. **matra Nadasia Kasaye**[4]

A. II.[5]

1. **sadha matra A[b]uholaa**
2. **pi[ta]mahi-Pishpasria bhra-**
3. **[t]ra Hayuarana sadha Hana-dhi[tra]**[6]
4. **a[te]urena**[7] **[a]rakapa-**[8]
5. rivarena iśe praḍhavipra[de]-
6. śe nisime śarira pra[ti]ṭhavito[9]

7. **bhakavata-Śakamunisa Budhasa [| *]**
8. **mukihitaya saspae bhusati [| *]**
9. **Thuva cha sagharamo cha chat[u]-**
10. **diśasa saghasa Sarva-**
11. **stivadana parigrahe [|| *].**

Translation.

I.

By *Nadasi Kasa*, the first queen of the great Satrap Rajula, the daughter of *Yasi Kamudha*, the mother of the Cæsar (*yurarâja*) *Kharaosta*,

II.

(*Who is associated*) with her mother *Abuhola*, her grandmother *Pishpasri* (*Viśvaśrî* ?), her brother *Hayuara*, her daughter *Hana*, (and) with the crowd of the women of the harem, has deposited in this spot of the earth, in the Stûpa (*nisima*), a relic of divine Śâkyamuni Buddha ; it will conduce to eternal welfare (*viz.*) liberation. Both the

Đại Chúng Bộ: Ma Ha Tăng Kỳ Bộ: Mahasanghika (skt). "The Wardak vase in Afghanistan containing the relics of the Buddha was presented to the teachers of the Mahasanghikas by one Kamalagulya during the reign of Huviska. At Andharah in Afghanistan, Hsuan-Tsang found three monasteries belonging to this sect, which proves that this sect was popular in the North-West. The cave at Karle in Maharashtra records the gift of a village as also of a nine-celled hall to the adherents of the school of the Mahasanghikas. Clearly, the Mahasanghikas had a center at Karle and exercised influence over the people of the West. They were not thus confined to Magadha alone, but spread over the northern and western parts of India and had adherents scattered all over the country."

Map showing interaction areas from Susa to Meluhha (Amri), 3rd millennium BCE aru m. sun ' (Sankrit) Yor id. (Khotanese) arka 'sun' (Sanskrit) Rebus: erka = ekke (Tbh. of arka) aka (Tbh. of arka) copper (metal); crystal (Kannada) cf. eruvai = copper (Tamil) eraka, er-aka = any metal infusion (Kannada.Tulu); erako molten cast (Tulu)

Indus seal.

aryā 'I' aryeh 'lion' (Aramaic), ari 'lion' (Hebrew), aria (Akkadian). Hari 'lion'

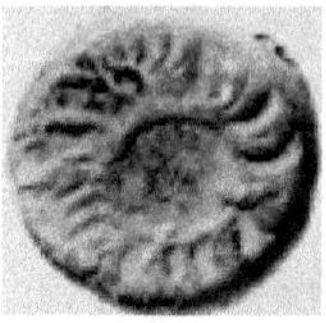

(Sanskrit) A lion; हरि hari-कान्त 'beautiful as a lion'; -मेधस् *m.* N. of Viṣṇu (Sanskrit) A Northwest Semitic root *ryh 'lion'. Rebus: ārya 'noble person, ārya speaker'. *Ari* was used in Hebrew as an honorific for an important man.

mēḍha 'The polar star' (Marathi). Rebus: meḍ 'metal'. mēdha मेधः 'an offering, an oblation'.

Early 6th century BC Lydian electrum coin (one-third stater denomination). KINGS of Lydia. Uncertain King. Early 6th century BC. EL Third Stater - Trite (4.71 gm). Head of roaring lion right, sun with multiple rays on forehead.

King Shalivahana demarcated *Sindhurāṣtra* as the land and nation of the Aryas that lay east of the Sindhu River effectively separating it from the land of the mlecchas on the west of the Sindhu River : *sthāpita tena maryāda mlecchāryānām prithak prithak. Sindhu sthānam iti jneyam rāṣṭram āryasya ca uttamam. Mleccha sthānam param sindhoh kritam tena mahātmanā* (Bhavishya Purāna Pratisarga adhyāya 2). Commenting on Jaiminisutra (1:3.10), Śabara raised and discussed the problem whether the meaning of certain Vedic words like pica or nema (which were not common among the Aryas but well known among the mlechhas) should be derived from Sanskrit roots or from their actual usage among the mlechhas. He advocated the linguistic usages of the mlecchas in secular matters and encouraged their incorporation at the Prakrit (lokavāni) level.

2nd century BCE silver drachm coin of the Kuninda king Amoghabhuti who ruled in the fertile valley of Yamuna, Beas and Sutlej rivers (modern Punjab in northern India). The legends on obverse reads *Rajnah Kunindasya Amoghabhutisya maharajasya*, in Brahmi. The reverse bears *Maharajasa* in Kharoṣṭī.

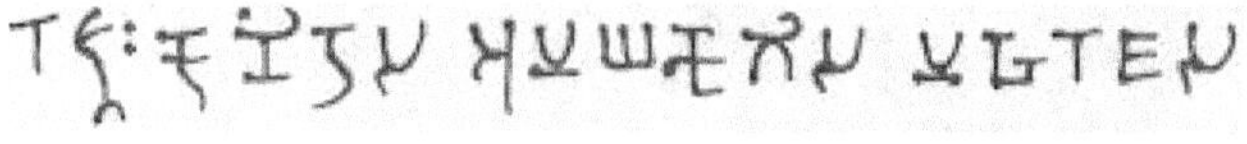

Brahmi script inscription on Kuninda coin (Obverse)

Kharoshthi script inscription on Kuninda coin (Reverse)

A *'Kuninda coin'* minted by Raja Amoghabhuti (late 2nd century BCE.

Obverse:[3] Deer facing female divinity, holding three ingot pellets. There are two mollusc symbols above the deer. The Brahmi legend reads from left to right: '*Rajna Kunindasa Amoghabhutisa Maharajasa'.* Reverse: Shows a Buddhist Stupa in the centre flanked by a tree-on-railing on the right and symbols - tamga and swastika on the left. The Kharoṣṭī script reads from right to left: *'Rana Kunidasa Amoghabhutisa Maharajasa'.* The region of Kuninda (also called Kulinda) stretched from the borders of Audumbara (c. 150-100 BCE) temporarily independent of the Punjab area in the Pathankot region of the Beas river valley to the borders of Nepal. Audumbara kings *Dharagosa* and *Rudravarma* were perhaps the first to introduce the Brahmi script on one side with the Kharoṣṭī script on the other side of their coins.

"The coins showing the Greek divinities - Zeus (holding a thunderbolt and/or a sceptre), Hercules (holding a club and/or lion skin), Nike (winged, City divinity holding cornucopia), Artemis drawing arrow from bow, Helios (Sun), Selene (Moon) and the Indo-Iranian divinities: Mozao Oaho or Mazdaonho (Ahura Mazda), Athasho (Fire), Bago (Bhaga), Miiro/ Mioro (Sun/Mithra), Ardoksho (Earth), Orlango (Verethaghna), Saorhora (Sherewar, Mao (Moon), Apto/Appo (Waters), Vado (Wind), Pharro (Aura /Khwarena), Manaobago (Vohu Manah), Boddo (Buddha), sometimes a humped Indian bull or an elephant or the two-humped Bactrian camel on the reverse...were slowly replaced by the standing Shiva (holding a trident or a club) in front of a bull, Parvati (consort of Shiva) seated on a lion, Lakshmi (representing wealth) seated or standing on a lotus, Peacock motif… The coins were minted mainly in Balkh, Merv, Herat, Pushkalavati (near modern Kabul), Takhshashila (modern Taxila), Bamiyan, Jammu..."

Demetrius (c.205-166 BCE) ruling in Arachosia (South Afghanistan) also minted bilingual coins, with Kharoṣṭī on the Reverse (maharajasa aparajitasa demetriyasa) and Greek on the Obverse (Invincible King Demetrius).

meḍ 'iron' has semantic cognates in Czech and Russian: měď (copper)(Czech) mid′ (copper, cuprum, orichalc)(Ukrainian) med′ (copper, cuprum, Cu), mednyy (copper, cupreous, brassy, brazen, brass), omednyat′ (copper, coppering), sul′fatmedi (Copper), politseyskiy (policeman, constable, peeler, policemen, redcap), pokryvat′ med′yu (copper), payal′nik (soldering iron, copper, soldering pen, soldering-iron), mednyy kotel (copper), medno-krasnyy (copper), mednaya moneta (copper). медь (copper, cuprum, Cu), медный (copper, cupreous, brassy, brazen, brass), омеднять (copper, coppering), Сульфатмеди (Copper), полицейский (policeman, constable, peeler, policemen, redcap), покрывать медью (copper), паяльник (soldering iron, copper, soldering pen, soldering-iron), медный котел (copper), медно-красный (copper), медная монета (copper).(Russian).

While a composite comparable glyph (Goat + fish) of the Uruk trough type has

not been identified in the corpus of Indus inscriptions, there are seals which show fish glyph together with antelope glyph; fish glyph together with composite bull + young bull calf glyph. The rebus readings of the hieroglyphs are: mẽḍha 'antelope'; rebus: meḍ 'iron' (Ho.) koḍiyum 'heifer'; rebus: koḍ 'artisan's workshop'. aya 'fish'; rebus: aya 'cast metal' (G.).

'How did my ancestors give names to objects?' asked Karmi Hatu, rhetorically and went on to cite the authority of part of the Rigveda Hymn 71 of Mandala 10. 'The Hymn also explains why Vāk divinity is associated with speech.

1. *bŕhaspate prathamáṃ vācó ágraṃ / yát praírata nāmadhéyaṃ dádhānāḥ*
yád eṣāṃ śréṣṭhaṃ yád ariprám âsīt / preṇâ tád eṣāṃ níhitaṃ gúhāvíḥ
2. *sáktum iva títa'unā punánto / yátra dhîrā mánasā vâcam ákrata*
yátrā sákhāyaḥ sakhyâni jānate / bhadraíṣāṃ lakṣmîr níhitâdhi vācí
3. *yajñéna vācáḥ padavîyam āyan / tâm ánv avindann ŕṣiṣu právíṣṭām*
tâm ābhŕtyā vy àdadhuḥ purutrâ / tâṃ saptá rebhâ abhí sáṃ navante
4. *utá tvaḥ páśyan ná dadarśa vâcam / utá tvaḥ śṛṇván ná śṛṇoty enām*
utó tvasmai tanvàṃ ví sasre / jāyéva pátya uśatî suvâsāḥ

"When men, Brihaspati!, giving names to objects, sent out Vāk's first and earliest utterances
All that was excellent and spotless, treasured within them, was disclosed through their affection."

"Where, like men cleansing corn-flour in a cribble, the wise in mind have created language,

Friends see and recognize the marks of friendship: their speech retains the blessed sign imprinted."

"With sacrifice the trace of Vāk they followed, and found her harbouring within the Rsis.

They brought her, dealt her forth in many places: seven singers make her tones resound in concert."

"One man hath ne'er seen Vāk, and yet he seeth: one man hath hearing but hath never heard her.

But to another hath she shown her beauty as a fond well-dressed woman to her husband."

Another part of Hymn 100 of Mandala 8 elaorates on divine form of Vāk'.

10. *yád vâg vádanty avicetanâni / râṣṭrī devânāṃ niṣasâda mandrâ*

cátasra ûrjaṃ duduhe páyāṃsi / kvà svid asyāḥ paramáṃ jagāma

11. *devîṃ vâcam ajanayanta devâs / tâṃ viśvárūpāḥ paśávo vadanti*

sâ no mandréṣam ûrjaṃ dúhānā / dhenúr vâg asmân úpa súṣṭutaítu

"When, uttering words which no one comprehended, Vāk, Queen of Gods, the Gladdener, was seated,

The heaven's four regions drew forth drink and vigour: now whither hath her noblest portion vanished?"

"The Deities generated Vāk the Goddess, and animals of every figure speak her.

May she, the Gladdener, yielding food and vigour, the Milch-cow Vāk, approach us meetly lauded."

Vāk, the divine Words flow like a river. Knowledge is her vehicle. She is the mother of fragrances, emotions. Gandharva and apsaras are her children. Books or musical instruments are abodes of the divine. She is the mother of the Vedas and contains all the worlds within herself. Vāk is everything says the *Aitareya Āraṇyaka* *Śabda*, speech is *nitya*, eternal, so is *sphoṭa*, *artha*, meaning – which is a permanent aspect of *Śabda*, *dhvani* or acoustics of *Śabda* us ephemeral, transient aspect. Hence the flow of language with variant pronunciations for the same word or *Śabda*, *Śabda*, as linguistic performance is the same as *brahman*. When carved in, she is called *brahmi*. Vāk is supreme, she is Rāṣṭrī, an Empress, a union of nations Rāṣṭram.

Harosheth hagoyim which means 'smithy of nations' yields a cognate word *kharoṣṭi*, a name for an ancient writing system. The cognate of *Harosheth*, the word *kharoṣṭi* can thus also be interpreted to mean 'smithy (carving).'

'We are dealing with the evolution of a writing system, invented by artisans for use by merchants and caravans of merchants,' said Karmi responding to ABC News Channel anchor, Catherine's query, 'So, how is Sarasvati related to invention of writing?'

Let us hear some words which are the tools of trade of ancestral metal-workers as we see the unambiguous orthography of two glyphs ligatured in the following seal: 1. *lo*, 'leaf'; 2. *khaṇḍá*, 'mountain-(pass)', thus, read together as *lo-khaṇḍ* to mean literally 'leaf-mountain-pass'; but read rebus to mean 'metalware': H. *lokhaṇḍ* m. iron tools, pots and pans '; N. *lokhar* bag in which a barber keeps his tools '; H. *lokhar* m. iron tools, pots and pans '; X *lauhabhāṇḍa* -- : Ku. *lokhaṛ* iron tools '; G. *lokhãḍ* n. tools, iron, ironware '; M. *lokhãḍ* n.

khaḍū ‘squirrel’. खडी [khaḍī] A squirrel. खडू [khaḍū] *f* खडूळ *f* A squirrel.

kaṇḍ = altar, furnace (Santali) लोहकारकन्दुः f. a blacksmith's smelting furnace (Grierson Kashmiri lex.) *payĕn-kōda* पयन्-कौँद। परिपाककन्दुः f. a kiln (a potter's, a lime-kiln, and brick-kiln, or the like); a furnace (for smelting)]. *kāndavika* = a baker; *kandu* = an iron plate or pan for baking cakes etc. (Kannada)

khaṇḍá hill, mountain pass' (< *rock ' < piece ' or < *pass ' < gap ': Gaw. *khaṇḍa* hill pasture '; Bshk. *khan* m. hill', Tor. *Khān* (Grierson) *khaṇḍ*, Mai. *khān*, Chil. Gau. *kān*, Phal. *khāṇ*, Sh. koh. *khŭṇ* m., gur. *khonn*, pales. *khōṇə*, jij. *khōṇ* mountain', gil. (Lor.) *kh̄* *ṇ* m. mountain pass'.

lōhá red, copper -- coloured ' ŚrS., made of copper ' ŚBr., m.n. copper ' VS., iron ' MBh. [*rudh --] Pa. *lōha* -- m. metal, esp. copper or bronze '; Pk. *lōha* -- m. iron ', Gy. pal. *li°*, *lihi*, obl. *elhás*, *loa* steel'; Kho. *loh* copper'; S. *lohu* m. iron ', L. *lohā* m., awāṇ. *lō`ā*, P. *lohā* m. (→ K.rām. ḍoḍ. *lohā*), WPah. *lõu* n., *lòtilde;* n., *lōh*, *luhā*, *lohā*, Ku. *luwā*, N. *lohu*, *°hā*, A. *lo*, B. *lo*, *no*, Or. *lohā*, *luhā*,

Mth. *loh*, Bhoj. *lohā*, Aw.lakh. *lōh*, H. *loh*, *lohā* m., G. M. *loh* n.; Si. *loho*, *lō* metal, ore, iron '; Md. *ratu* -- *lō* copper '.

‘The occurrence of phonetic variants *lo*, *no*, meaning ‘copper’ in Bengali is instructive,’ noted Karmi Hatu that a word *no* meaning ‘nine’ could earlier have been pronounced *lo* ‘nine’. This semantic of *lo* ‘nine’ is used to reinforce the message that the intended word in an extraordinary orthographic composition on a seal is *lo* ‘nine, leaf’; read rebus *lo* 'metal'. The reinforcement of the hieroglyphic message is conveyed orthographically by depicting nine leaves ! Let us count the leaves, they are seven on the top branch and two on the bottom branch totaling nine, all leaf stems emanating from a portable furnace or gimlet, in a stylized artwork depicting a tuner-casting-metalsmith's workshop,' noted Karmi, counting the leaves one by one on the following seal shown to the ABC News Channel viewers:

The pair of one-horned bull calves with pronounced rings on the neck are read literally, *dula* 'pair', *koḍe* 'bull calf', *koḍiyum* 'rings on neck', which together read rebus *dul koḍ* 'casting (metal) workshop'.

kandhi = a lump, a piece (Santali) [The circle thus connotes an ingot taken out of a *kaṇḍ*, 'furnace']. *kāndavika* = a baker; *kandu* = an iron plate or pan for baking cakes etc. (Kannada) *khāṇḍā* 'notch'; rebus: *kaṇḍ*, 'furnace'.

kuṛy Hindu temple (Toda) *kuṛm* family; *kuḍḷ* front room of house; *kuṛḷ* hut; *guṛy* temple (Kota)

kaṇḍ = altar, furnace (Santali) लोहकारकन्दुः f. a blacksmith's smelting furnace (Grierson Kashmiri lex.) payĕn-kōda पयन्-कौँद। परिपाककन्दुः f. a kiln (a potter's, a lime-kiln, and brick-kiln, or the like); a furnace (for smelting) This yajn~a kuṇḍam can be denoted rebus, by perforated beads (kandi) or on ivory (khaṇḍ):

kaḍī a chain; a hook; a link (G.); kaḍum a bracelet, a ring (G.) Rebus: kaḍiyo [Hem. Des. kaḍaio = Skt. sthapati a mason] a bricklayer; a mason; kaḍiyaṇa, kaḍiyeṇa a woman of the bricklayer caste; a wife of a bricklayer (G.)

kandi 'hole, opening' (Ka.) kandi (pl. -l) beads, necklace (Pa.); kanti (pl. -l) bead, (pl.) necklace; kandit. bead (Ga.)

kuṇḍa n. clump' e.g. darbha—kuṇḍa—Pāṇ. Kundār turner (A.) kuṇḍī = crooked buffalo horns (L.) rebus: kuṇḍī = chief of village. Kuṇḍi-a = village headman; leader of a village (Pkt.lex.) I.e. śreṇi jeṭṭha chief of metal-worker guild.

Glyphics of shoggy, brisltles of hair on the face of the person: Shoggy hair; tiger's mane. Sodo bodo, sodro bodro adj. adv. Rough, hairy, shoggy, hirsute, uneven; sodo [Persian. Sodā, dealing] trade; traffic; merchandise; marketing; a bargain; the purchase or sale of goods; buying and selling; mercantile dealings (G.lex.) sodagor = a merchant, trader; sodāgor (P.B.) (Santali.lex.)

On the Sharkalisharri cylinder, fifth king of the Akkad dynasty, two naked heroes, acolytes of Eas, water two buffaloes which carry the inscription, central element of the composition: "the divine Sharkalisharri, king of Akkad, Ibni-sharrum, the scribe, (is) his servant." – Louvre Fine engraving, elegant drawing, and a balanced composition make this seal one of the masterpieces of glyptic art. The decoration, which is characteristic of the Agade period, shows two buffaloes that have just slaked their thirst in the stream of water spurting from two vases held by two naked kneeling heroes. A masterpiece of glyptic art

This seal, which belonged to Ibni-Sharrum, the scribe of King Sharkali-Sharri, who succeeded his father Naram-Sin, is one of the most striking examples of the perfection attained by carvers in the Agade period. The two naked, curly-headed heroes are arranged symmetrically, half-kneeling. They are both holding vases from which water is gushing as a symbol of fertility and abundance; it is also the attribute of the god of the river, Enki-Ea, of whom these spirits of running water are indeed the acolytes. Two arni, or water buffaloes, have just drunk from them. Below the scene, a river winds between the mountains represented conventionally by a pattern of two lines of scales. The central cartouche bearing an inscription is held between the buffaloes' horns.

A scene testifying to relations with distant lands

Buffaloes are emblematic animals in glyptic art in the Agade period. They first appear in the reign of Sargon, indicating sustained relations between the Akkadian Empire and the distant country of Meluhha, that is, the present Indus Valley, where these animals come from. These exotic creatures were probably kept in zoos and do not seem to have been acclimatized in Iraq at the end of the 3rd millennium BC. Indeed, it was not until the Sassanid Empire that they reappeared. The engraver has carefully accentuated the animals' powerful muscles and spectacular horns, which are shown as if seen from above, as they appear on the seals of the Indus.

The production of a royal workshop

The calm balance of the composition, based on horizontal and vertical lines, gives this in low relief a classical monumental character, typical of the style of the late Akkadian period. Seals of this quality were the preserve of the entourage of the royal family or high dignitaries and were probably made in a workshop whose production was reserved for this elite.

The cylinder seal belonged to Ibni-sharrum, a scribe of Shar-kalisharri and is now in the Louvre Museum. The inscription reads "O divine Shar-kali-sharri, Ibni-sharrum the scribe is your servant." Made of diorite or chlorite, the seal is dated to circa 2217-2193 BCE.

'Apart from the cuneiform inscription within a cartouche, what do the pictographs – flowing water and buffalo -- say? *lo kaḍ* !' Karmi Hatu raised her voice as she repeated, '*lo kaḍ*' and added,'Pay close attention to the artistic detail and orthography of the exquisite cylinder seal. At the bottom register, we find flowing waters signifying that the scribe Ibni-sharrum is from across the waters, the Persian gulf and the rivers, Sindhu (Indus) and Sarasvati. Look at the kneeling scribe's hairdo. There are six clear distinct curls of hair. I will demonstrate to you the significance of the number six and the six locks of hair – three on either side of the head -- in the same Indus language which was used to convey the words, *lo kaḍ* literally meaning 'flow of water' and 'buffalo,' rebus readings to mean 'metal-ware'. Clearly, Ibni-sharrum was a scribe from Meluhha who had also mastered the Akkadian writing system of cuneiform script. Pictographs as hieroglyphs were the medium of the Indus script which has been deployed on this bilingual cylinder seal. Sharkalisharri was the fifth king of the Akkad dynasty. The hieroglyph of a pot overflowing with water occurs on an equally exquite pectoral of Mohenjodaro. Take a look.'

The imageries of overflowing pot are seen in other examples found in the British Museum. Clay relief stamped with the figure of the Babylonian hero Gilgamesh, holding a vase from which two streams of water flow. (British Museum No. 21204)

Fragment of limestone sculptured in relief with vases from which streams of water flow. (British Museum No. 95477)

Then, Karmi Hatu presented this pectoral image to the ABC News channel viewers:

Karmi Hatu continued the explanation, 'This is a hieroglyph of an overflowing pot, together with the glyphs of one-horned young bull calf and standard device. Now let me present the readings of the hieroglyph of overflowing pot. We have already seen the Indus language elaborations for the one-horned young bull calf and standard device which denote the turner-workshop-treasure-guard, *kundar koḍ jangāḍiyo.* We have already seen that the narrow-necked rim of jar is denoted by the words *kaṇḍa kanka,* the rebus reading of which conveys the meaning, 'furnace-scribe.' Now, let us repeat the words connoting the pictorial of 'overflowing' pot.'

<lo->(B) {V} ``(pot, etc.) to ^overflow''. See <lo-> `to be left over'. (Munda etyma) Rebus: <lua>(B), <loa>(B) {N} ``^iron''. Pl. <-le>. <lowa>(F) {N} ``^iron''.

kaḍun -- कडुन् । ईषत्पाकयोजनया जलनिःसारणम् m.inf. to pour or strain off the water (in which food has been cooked).

Cylinder seal impression, circa Proto-Elamite period.

Nude Bearded Hero Wrestling with Water Buffalo; Bull Man Fighting Lion Cylinder seal and impression Mesopotamia, Akkadian period (ca. 2334–2154 B.C.)

Serpentine 'What a surprise ! We find on this cylinder seal, the fighting figures flank a pictograph of mountain-passes ligatured to an artistically stylized ficus-leaf, the same way a hieroglyph on a Kalibangan seal showed *lo khaṇḍ* meaning literally 'ficus leaf mountain-pass' read rebus to convey 'metalware'. 'It is clear,'

Karmi emphasized, 'that the pictographs used on the Kalibangan seal and the two cylinder seals of Akkad were meaningful, literate hieroglyphs inscribed by scribes. Akkadian scribes had borrowed and deployed the Indus script hieroglyphs. Now, tell me where was writing invented, circa 3500 BCE?' Karmi paused with this rhetorical question and did not wait for an answer from the ABC News channel anchor, Catherine. 'I say, Sarasvati river basin, where Meluhha, *Mleccha vācas* was spoken and where Indus script was invented. Anyway, let the viewers decide,' Karmi said, almost *sotto voce*.

Chapter 22 Importance of a count of 'six'

Elamite lady spinner. Musee du Louvre. Paris. An elegantly coiffed, exquisitely-dressed and well fanned Elamite woman sits on a feline footed stool winding thread on a spindle. The stool on which the lovely Elamite lady sits has the legs of a feline; the fish is also placed on a similar stool in front her.This five-inch fragment is dated 8th century BCE. It was molded and carved from a mix of bitumen, ground calcite, and quartz. The Elamites used bitumen, a naturally occurring mineral pitch, or asphalt, for vessels, sculpture, glue, caulking, and waterproofing.

http://www.oznet.net/iran/elamspin.htm

The glyphics represent *kol khũṭ khati,* 'working in iron, a guild of wheelwrights '

kola 'tiger' (Telugu); rebus: kol 'working in iron (Tamil). The legs of the two stools shows glyphic of tiger's foot. Glyph: 'foot, hoof': Glyph: 'hoof': Ku. *khuṭo* leg, foot ', *°ṭī* goat's leg '; N. *khuṭo* leg, foot '(CDIAL 3894). S. *khuṛī* f. heel '; WPah. paṅ. *khūṛ* foot '. khura m. hoof ' KātyŚr̥. 2. *khuḍa -- 1 (*khuḍaka* -- , *khula°* ankle -- bone ' Suśr.). [← Drav. T. Burrow BSOAS xii 376: it belongs to the word -- group heel <-> ankle -- knee -- wrist ', see *kuṭṭha --](CDIAL 3906). *Ta.* kuracu, kuraccai horse's hoof. *Ka.* gorasu, gorase, gorise, gorusu hoof. *Te.* gorija, gorise, (B. also) gorije, korije id. / Cf. Skt.khura- id. (DEDR 1770). Allograph: (Kathiawar) *khũṭ* m. Brahmani bull ' (G.) Rebus: *khũṭ* 'community, guild' (Santali)

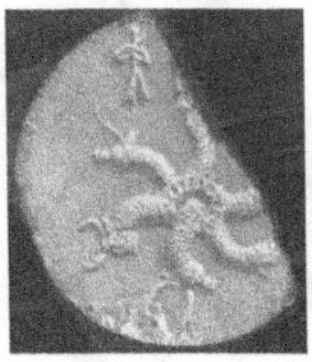

Glyph: kātī 'spinner' (G.) Rebus: khati 'wheelwright' (H.) kāṭi = fireplace in the form of a long ditch (Ta.Skt.Vedic) kāṭya = being in a hole (VS. XVI.37); kāṭ a hole, depth (RV. i. 106.6) khāḍ a ditch, a trench; khāḍ o khaiyo several pits and ditches (G.) khaṇḍrun: 'pit (furnace)' (Santali)

ayo 'fish' (Mu.); rebus: aya 'metal' (G.)

Glyphic: 'count of six': bhaṭa 'six' (G.); rebus: bhaṭa 'furnace' (Santali) kola 'woman' (Nahali); Rebus: kolami 'smithy' (Te.) Vikalpa: goti 'woman'; rebus; goṭ 'cow-pen'; rebus: koḍ 'place where artisans work' (Kuwi) Kur. kaṇḍō a stool. Malt. kanḍo stool, seat. (DEDR 1179) Rebus: kaṇḍ 'fire-altar, furnace' (Santali) kola 'tiger, jackal' (Kon.); rebus: kolami 'smithy' (Te.) Grapheme as a phonetic determinant of the depiction of woman, kola; rebus: kolami 'smithy' (Te.)

m417 six heads from a core bhaṭa 'six' (G.) rebus: baṭa = kiln (Santali); baṭa = a kind of iron (G.) bhaṭṭhī f. 'kiln, distillery', awāṇ. bhaṭh; P. bhaṭṭh m., °ṭhī f. 'furnace', bhaṭṭhā m. 'kiln'; S. bhaṭṭhī keṇī 'distil (spirits) Glyph: 'animals': asaramu, pasalamu = an animal, a beast, a brute, quadruped (Te.) Rebus: pasra = a smithy, place where a black-smith works, to work as a blacksmith; kamar pasra = a smithy; pasrao lagao akata se ban:? Has the blacksmith begun to work? pasraedae = the blacksmith is at his work (Santali.lex.) pasra 'smithy' (Santali) pasra meṛed, pasāra meṛed = syn. of koṭe meṛed = forged iron, in contrast to dul meṛed, cast iron (Mundari.)

bhaṭa 'six' (G.) Rebus: bhaṭa 'furnace' (G.)

kola 'woman' (Nahali); Rebus: kolami 'smithy' (Te.)

meḍhi, miḍhī, meṇḍhī = a plait in a woman's hair; a plaited or twisted strand of hair (P.) मेढा [mēḍhā] meṇḍa A twist or tangle arising in thread or cord, a curl or snarl. (Marathi) (CDIAL 10312). The cylinder seal in British Museum. A count of six locks of hair on the bearded person in the middle grappling with and flanked

by holding apart two one-horned young bull calves.

Mohenjodaro seal. Person grappling with two flanking tigers standing and rearing on their hindlegs. Comparable to the Mesopotamian cylinder seal, this Indus seal depicts a person with six hair-knots.

Scarf as an Indus script hieroglyph

Scarf is carried in a procession depicted on a terracotta tablet (together with a banner showing a one-horned heifer and a portable standard device).

Scarf is ligatured as a pigtail to a standing, horned person within a pot decorated with ficus leaves as a torana.

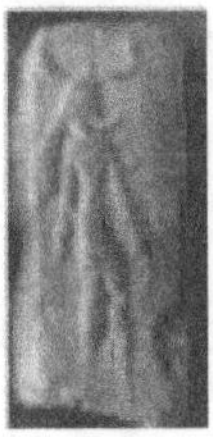

Scarf shown ligatured as a pigtail to a horned, standing person. Tablet (One side of a prism tablet).

A glyphic element

ligatured to a horned, kneeling person in front of a horned, standing person (also with scarf as a hieroglyph) within a torana. One side of a tablet.

er-agu = a bow, an obeisance; er-aguha = bowing, coming down; er-agisu = to bow, to be bent; to make obeisance to; to crouch; to come down; to alight (Kannada) erugu = to bow, to salute or make obeisance (Telugu) Rebus: eraka 'copper' (Kannada) erka = (Tbh. Of arka) copper (metal); crystal (Kannada) eraka, er-aka = any metal infusion (Kannada.Tulu) eruvai 'copper' (Tamil); ere dark red (Kannada) Er-r-a = red; (arka-) agasāle, agasāli, agasālavāḍu = a goldsmith (Telugu)

Thus, the horned, scarfed, kneeling person is read rebus: *eraka dhatu* 'copper mineral'.

Decoding 'scarf' glyph: dhaṭu m. (also dhaṭhu) m. 'scarf' (WPah.) Rebus: dhatu 'minerals' (Santali)
Importance of *Bos gaurus*

Person throwing a spear at a buffalo and placing one foot on the head of the buffalo. *kolsa* = to kick the foot forward, the foot to come into contact with anything when walking or running; *kolsa pasirkedan* = I kicked it over (Santali.lex.) *kola* = killing, e.g. *āḍukola* = woman-slaying (Te.) Thus, *homa kola* = bison slaying. Rebus: hom = gold (Ka.) *kol*=metal (Ta.)

kwal.el 'smithy, temple in Kota village' (Kota); kwala.l Kota smithy (Toda) Vikalpa: mēṛsa = v.a. toss, kick with the foot, hit with the tail (Santali)

Rebus: *mẽṛhẽt* iron; *ispat mẽṛhẽt* = steel; *dul mẽṛhẽt* = cast iron (Munda.); *meḍ 'iron'* (Ho.)

Impression of an Indus-style cylinder seal of unknown Near Eastern origin in the Musee du Louvre, Paris. One of the two anthropomorphic figures carved on this seal wears the horns of water buffalo while sitting on a throne with hoofed legs, surrounded by snakes, fishes and water buffaloes. Copyrighted photo by M. Chuzeville for the Departement des antiquites orientales, Musee du Louvre.

A pair of buffaloes flank a round spot in the bottom register of the cylinder seal impression.

Glyph: 'round spot': गोटी [gōṭī] f (Dim. Of गोटा) A roundish stone or pebble. Rebus: कोठी [kōṭhī] f (कोष्ट S) A granary, garner, storehouse, warehouse, treasury, factory, bank. (Marathi)

Decoding rebus other hieroglyphs of the cylinder seal

kaṭa-sal 'buffalo'. Rebus: kaḍacal 'turner's workshop'. meḍh 'ram'. Rebus: meḍ 'iron'. Badhoe 'boar'. Rebus: baḍhi 'worker in wood and iron'. aya 'fish'. Rebus: aya 'metal'. pajhaṛ 'kite'. Rebus: pasra 'smithy'. kuṭi 'tree'. Rebus: kuṭhi 'smelter'. tagaraka 'taberna montana' (five-petalled flower). Rebus: tagara 'tin'. dula kola 'pair of tigers'. Rebus: dul kol 'casting work in iron'. kola 'woman'. Rebus: kolami 'smithy/forge'. ṭhaṭera 'buffalo horns'. ṭhaṭera 'brass worker'. kaṇḍo 'stool'. Rebus: kaṇḍ 'furnace, altar'.

This is a veritable inventory, a catalog of bronze-age repertoire of the Indus artisans' workshop.

Ligature, a technique used by scribes/artisans of the civilization

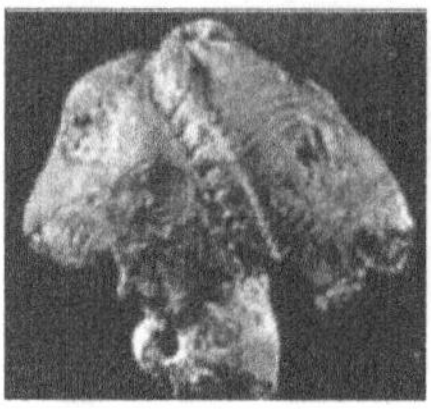  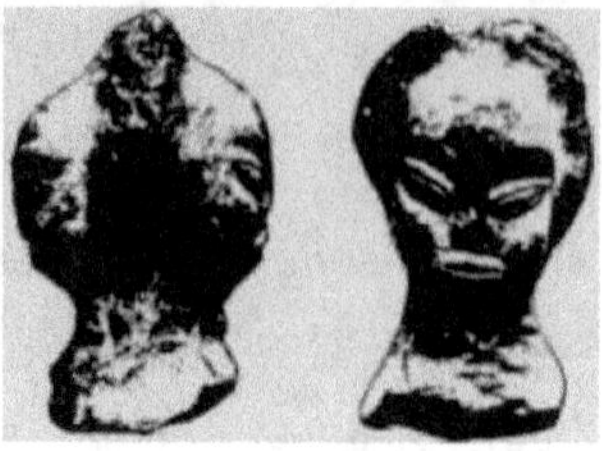

Ligatured sculpture: three-faced: tiger, bovine, elephant, Nausharo NS 92.02.70.04 6.76 cm (h); three-headed: elephant, buffalo, bottom jaw of a feline. NS 91.02.32.01.LXXXII. Dept. of Archaeology, Karachi. EBK 7712. The glyphs of elephant, buffalo and tiger occur on Mohenjo-daro Seal m0304. The glyphic compositions (pictographs + text glyphs) have been explained to be a detailed account of the metal work engaged in by the Indus artisans.

Elephant: ibha (glyph). Rebus: ibbo (merchant of ib 'iron')

Tiger: kola (glyph). Rebus: kol (working in iron, kolami 'smithy/forge')

Buffalo: kaṭā, kaṭamā 'bison' (Ta.)(DEDR 1114) (glyph). Rebus: kaḍiyo [Hem. Des. kaḍa-i-o = (Skt. Sthapati, a mason) a bricklayer, mason (G.)]

A ligatured glyph wad used to connote the professional competence of an artisan who performed the roles of merchant, smith and mason.

h1971B Harappa. Three tablets with identical glyphic compositions on both sides: h1970, h1971 and h1972. Seated figure or deity with reed house or shrine at one side. Left: H95-2524; Right: H95-2487.

Harappa. Planoconvex molded tablet found on Mound ET. A. Reverse. a female

deity battling two tigers and standing above an elephant and below a six-spoked wheel; b. Obverse. A person spearing with a barbed spear a buffalo in front of a seated horned deity wearing bangles and with a plumed headdress. The person presses his foot down the buffalo's head. An alligator with a narrow snout is on the top register. "We have found two other broken tablets at Harappa that appear to have been made from the same

mold that was used to create the scene of a deity battling two tigers and standing above an elephant. One was found in a room located on the southern slope of Mount ET in 1996 and another example comes from excavations on Mound F in the 1930s. However, the flat obverse of both of these broken tablets does not show the spearing of a buffalo, rather it depicts the more well-known scene showing a tiger looking back over its shoulder at a person sitting on the branch of a tree. Several other flat or twisted rectangular terracotta tablets found at Harappa combine these two narrative scenes of a figure strangling two tigers on one side of a tablet, and the tiger looking back over its shoulder at a figure in a tree on the other side." [JM Kenoyer, 1998, p. 115].

kolmo 'rice plant' (Mu.) Rebus: kolami 'furnace,smithy' (Te.) Vikalpa: pajhaṛ = to sprout from a root (Santali); Rebus: pasra 'smithy, forge' (Santali)

dhaṭu m. (also dhaṭhu) m. 'scarf' (Wpah.) (CDIAL 6707)Rebus: dhatu 'minerals' (Santali)

pattar 'trough'; pattar 'merchant':

bull *ḍaṅgar* ṭhākur blacksmith (Mth.)

buffalp *sal kaḍa* 'casting workshop of *kaḍa-i-o,* 'turner, mason'.

elephant ibha, karibha karba 'iron'; ib 'iron'

kola 'tiger' (Telugu); कोल्हा kōlhā kolo, koleā 'jackal' (Kon.Santali); rebus: kol 'working in iron (Tamil) : kol pañcaloha 'five metals'(Ta.); kol 'furnace, forge' (Kuwi) kolhali to forge (Ko.)

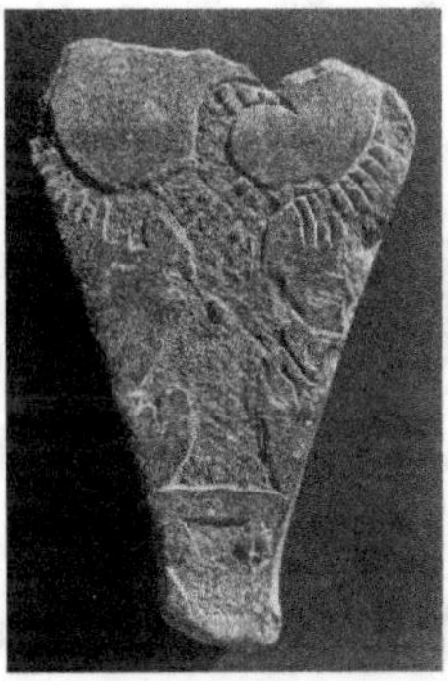

Or. *gaṇḍā. kāṇḍ* 'stone/nodule (metal)'.

meḍho a ram, a sheep (G.) miṇḍāl markhor (Tor.wali) meḍ iron (Ho.)

ranku 'tin' (Santali) ranku 'liquid measure' (Santali) ranku 'antelope' (Santali) Inscribed on two pure tin

eruvai = copper (Ta.lex.) eraka, er-aka = any metal infusion (Ka.Tu.); erako molten cast (Tu.lex.) *Ta.* eruvai blood, (?) copper.

Ta. eruvai a kind of kite whose head is white and whose body is brown; eagle. *Ma.* eruva eagle, kite. Akkadian eru 'eagle'. Akkadian aru/eru may be equivalent of the Hebrew 'rh 'eagle'. ru 'eagle'. Bab. also vulture? āru(m) 'warrior'.

Tepe yahya. Eagle on both sides of a ceremonial chlorite axe head

Zu as a lion-headed eagle, ca. 2550–2500 BC, Louvre.

Bird Imdugud (Sumerian) or Anzû (Akkadian) stole the Tablets of Destiny from sky god Enlil.

Shoggy hair; tiger's mane. *Sodo bodo, sodro bodro* adj. adv. Rough, hairy, shoggy, hirsute, uneven; *sodo* [Persian. *Sodā*, dealing] trade; traffic; merchandise; marketing; a bargain; the purchase or sale of goods; buying and selling; mercantile dealings (G.lex.) sodagor = a merchant, trader;

Water-carrier glyph

kuṭi 'water-carrier' (Telugu); Rebus: kuṭhi 'smelter furnace' (Santali) kuṛī f. 'fireplace' (Hindi)

'Why have you presented all this evidence?' asked a juror.

Sagan kept silent, hoping that it is for the juror's and the judge to come to their own conclusions that he did not commit any crime of forgery and that the rim of jar was an important glyph left for posterity to ponder on the contributions made by early brassworker guilds on the banks of River Sarasvati.

Chapter 23 The mystery of Soma, ancu

I reported about Sagan's encounter with Chinese guards when he trekked up Muztagh Ata and did not complete the narrative.

I have reserved a report on the real reason for Sagan's visit to Muztagh Ata for this last chapter.

The reason was that he was seeking Ancu mentioned in a Tocharian lexicon.

When he returned from his trek on Muztagh Ata, he told mee that he found other seekers of ancu who had arrived from many parts of the world.

Sagan explained as we landed in Orlando when the court was closed for the Easter Spring break, 'Let me tell you why I trekked up Muztagh Ata and left you in the base camp. It has been an abiding passion of my life to contribute to my brassworkers' guild with information about the real identity of Soma.'

'Soma yajña performed for millennia on the banks of River Sarasvati?' I asked.

'Yes, the same soma. When my father taught me and Karmi Hatu the secret processes involved in alloying copper with zinc or tin to make sure that the alloyed metal was of the Jagadhri brass and bronze standards, he would recite rica-s from the Rigveda. We did not understand the significance of the chanting of mantras.' Sagan was in a pensive mood as tears rolled down his cheeks. This emotional outburst always occurs when Sagan remembers his father.

The Animal Kingdom was busy with pilgrims to the magic recreated recollecting some of the wonders of life on the globe.

The Kali river rapids queues were long and the wait time was 30 minutes without Fast Pass.

We had a pleasant surprise awaiting us as we relished the funnel cake we purchased in the park.

Sagan was ahead of me in the queue and just behind me was Judge Sarsuti. She was accompanied by a young boy and a young girl. Apparently she was taking her children for enjoying the vacation in the Disney world.

Suddenly, Judge Sarsuti and her children left the queue and moved towards the exit gate. I head her telling her children, ‘Let us take the Mount Everest ride first and then return to the Kali rapids.’

Sagan and I sat together on the Kali rapids boat. As the waters splashed over us, Sagan cried aloud, ‘Mā Sarasvati. Remember, that it was on the banks of River Sarasvati that our ancestors performed the atirātra soma yajñas continuously for five days and nights.’

The splashing of the waters of Kali Rapids tooks us down the memory lane of Balarama's pilgrimage along the River Sarasvati narrated in detail in the śalya parva of Mahabharata.

I told Sagan, ‘Yes, the waters of Kali help us recollect the prayers offered by Balarama to his ancestors when he visited Prthudaka before proceeding to Kurukshetra to watch the duel of *gadā yuddha* between Duryodhana and Bhima.’

‘What indeed was Soma?’ Sagan asked.

I told Sagan about the book titled *Indus writing in ancient Near East* which provides some leads which could unravel the mysterious identity of soma. The lead is provided by the narrative of Anzu in Sumeria. This Anzu is the same eagle Suparṇi of vedic tradition. The eagle finds the tablet hidden in the mountains of Mujavant. Seekers of ancu end up in Muztagh Ata which was referred to as Mujavant in Rigveda. The tablet the eagle finds contains the secret alchemical processes which wold transmute ancu 'iron' mentioned in Tocharian lexicons into electrum. Electrum was a gold-silver compound which had exchange value for the kayanides, the kavi-s. Sumerians renamed ancu of Tocharian as Anzu in Sumerian. In the vedic tradition, ancu continued to be referred to as amśu. This amśu was the cipher. Amśu were explained by Rigvedic rishi-s metaphorically as filaments to be filtered after pounding the rocks (plants) of Mujavant. Traders from Mujavant would bring in truck-loads of the mineral rocks and stones and the rishi-s would bargain and settle the exchange value for the amśu. The amśu is subjected to a filtering process in the filter called pavitram, 'sacred'. The amśu filaments yielded soma, the molten electrum. No soma substitute can replace the ancu of Muztagh Ata to get the desired yield of electrum. With any substitute, only the mantra-s will resound which contain the secret formula of alchemical transmutation by adding chosen herbal plants.

Recall how the Mundas and Assurs of Bastar identify tin-bearing cassiterite stones.

'Leaves of the sarai tree (*shorea robusta*) growing on tin-rich ground are often covered in yellow spots. Do you know the reason why? The leaves were found to contain 700 ppm of tin on analysis! Once such trees of shorea robusta are located, the next step is to dig into the ground to bring out cassiterite stones which can be smelted to yield tin. The key is to find the trees comparable to sarai trees which can bring out the soma from the rocks of Muztagh Ata.' I summarized to Sagan and showed him a geologist's report.

This sarai tree referred to by the metal workers of Bastar is calle sarja in Sanskrit. The word is cognate with Tamil *āccā*, 'shorea robusta' which yields the amśu resin. The early word is likely to be **sārc/j* which can explain the derivation of the word in Indian *sprachbund*. It is a matter for further research if *sajjī* f. 'the salsola plant (from which alkali natron is made)' of Lahnda and *sājī, sājī -- māṭi* 'natron, fuller's earth', of Bengali are relatable to the alkalis used to oxidize baser metals from the stone ores of Muztagh Ata. Remember that another name for shorea robusta is that it yields *rāḷa* ' tar, yellow resin '(Oriya), a yellow resin which could add hardness and add yellowish tinge to some minerals.

Sagan and I sat in sheer amazement at the wisdom of the metallurgists of Bastar who have been, generation after generation, digging and panning for the material wealth offered by mother earth using the signals nature sends out to carry out the processing steps of the type carried out for soma processing using 1500 degrees centigrade fire provided by the sacred vedi.

Ta. āccā sāl, *Shorea robusta*. Ka. āsu, āca, ārse the sal tree, S. robusta Roxb.(DEDR 343)

This word āccā from Tamil and word acchāvākaḥ of Vedic times give the ligatured clue, like the ligatured clues in hieroglyphs of Indus writing.

अच्छावाकः [अच्छं निर्मलं अच्छ आभिमुख्येन वा वक्ति शंसति; वच् कर्तरि संज्ञायां घञ् निपातस्य चेति दीर्घः Tv.] The invoker or inviter, a priest or Ṛitvij who is employed at Soma sacrifices, and is a co-adjutor of होतृ. Each of the four principal priests, होतृ, अध्वर्यु, उद्गातृ and ब्रह्मन् has three assistants, the total number of priests employed at Soma sacrifices being therefore 16; °सामन् *a.* N. of the Sāman to be chanted by an अच्छावाक, also called उद्वंशीय.

Branches of āccā sāl, *Shorea robusta*. of Muztagh Ata mixed with the stone ores containing an admixture of electrum together with iron and other mineralks would yield the clue to the efficient alchemical output of pure electrum.

After this excursus into the integrated nature of metallurgical and botanical phenomena which may explain the importanc e of identifying the stone ores from Muztagh Ata, Sagan was convinced that other seekers have missed out because they missed out that the clue is not in the rocks but in the yellow resin of āccā sāl, *shorea robusta*. This leaves two more clues to be resolved successfully. The first clue relates to *vasativari* waters of River Sarasvati. The second relates to the three stalks (of three trees?) exhibited on Sit Shamshi bronze which depicts a prayer to the Akkadian rising sun the way the rishi-s of yore offered their daily prayers of *sandhyāvandanam*. To start with, Sagan decided to mount a botanical expedition to Muztagh Ata.

After our raft ride on the Kali rapids, we moved on to the Bird show park of the Animal Kingdom in the Disney World of Orland. Sagan and I were surprised to find a pair of *anser indicus*. We found also Judge Sarsuti and her children watching the amazing show of trained birds. I can't explain why Judge Sarsuti also decided to visit the park during the spring break. Judges also have their families to care for while performing the duty of upholding the justice system. As I walked by the replica of the Kali mandir, I realized that search for truth is a life-mission.

Chapter 24 Epilogue

This is the opening for the story. I set out to tell an unusual love story of a pair of monogamous *Anser indicus*, Anserini of the family Anatidae (geese or hamsa), who visit Himalayas flying across Europe and relating their adventures while learning European languages and Indian languages. This remarkable behavior of monogamy by the geese made me realize that they exhibited unique human characteristics of leading a family life, living together as husband and wife. I was no ornithologist to document the behavior of the pair of geese toward the goslings and about the education and upbringing of the goslings.

I also forgot to document the amazing migratory path of *Anser indicus*. They cross the Himalayan heights migrating south from Russia, Kazakhstan, Mongolia and Tibet. There are disturbing reports that the birds are subject to predation from foxes, ravens, sea eagles and gulls. *Anser indicus* has bee sighted, according to unverified reports, flying over Mount Everest (8848 m.) and Mount Makalu (8481m.) making it the highest flying bird on the globe. Physiologistsand naturalists have been baffled by the migratory paths of *Anser indicus*. Black and Tenner evaluated oxygen transport in high altitude and wondered, 'there must be a good explanation for why the birds fly to the extreme altitudes…particularly since there are passes through the Himalaya at lower altitudes, and which are used by other migrating bird species.' They have the capacity to extract oxygen from hypoxic air and transport oxygen to the muscle fibres to sustain their flights, flapping hard to keep the lift in thin air.

I can speculate with Sagan, without having to provide footnotes of authorities, 'The past avatārs of hamsa might have been part of the gaṇa 'entourage' of Śiva meditating on Mount Kailas. *Anser indicus* are very sociable, with their wide wing area.'

Their flight across Himalaya is non-stop and they achieve the climbs over many Himalayan summits in only seven hours. What has baffled the scientists is that though tail winds rip apart the Himalayan rocks, *Anser indicus* just spurn the winds.

Anser indicus migrate from Kyrgyzstan, stopping over in western Tibet and southern Tajikistan for about 25 days and move further south because they spend the winter in the habitats of cultivated fields of southern regions of Asian continent – of Assam and Tamil Nadu, feeding on barley, rice nd wheat. They choose to nest on the Tibetan plateau.

In the Indian tradition, a sage who has sacrificed his worldly desires and taken to *sanyāsa* 'life of an ascetic' is revered to as a person who has attained *siddhi.* Such a siddha is called Paramahamsa, the Indian word for 'Supreme hamsa or *Anser indicus'.*

The Indian tradition respects the distinct stages of life – childhood, when a growing child is entirely dependent on parental and family care; student life, learning from the guru; married life and bringing up a family acquiring material benefits for living; *vānaprastha*, old age retired life but being cared for by the younger generations in the family; and lastly, *sanyāsa*, a stage when all material longings and family affections are given up or sacrificed and the pilgrim sets on a journey to understand the nature of the *paramātman,* sometimes also called Brahman, the Supreme Divine. Life journey itself is presented in these stages of life as *āśrama dharma. Āśrama* itself is a very difficult word to translate. It can simply be visualized as one of the stages of a human being's life journey. I could not account for these *āśrama* in the life of the husband-wife pair of hamsa which regularly visited the Himalayan summits including Mount Kailas. So, I gave up the idea of narrating the life of the pair of hamsa and also because the hamsa represented an undefined stage beyond *sanyāsa* almost like an after-life in a new *avatār*, changing from human body to assume the body of a bird.

Underlying the love story of Sagan Muṇḍa and Karmi Hatu is the story of Indian civilization formed for millennia at least from 6500 BCE which is an archaeologically attested date of the find of *śankha* (*turbinella pyrum*) shell bangle found in the burial of a woman at Mehergarh. Even today, we find that *śankha* bangle is a mandatory requirement for the bride in a Bengali or Oriya marriage, Today, the *śankha* is obtained from the coast near Surat (which also is a major center for processing and cutting diamonds) and Kīṟakkarai about ten kilometers from Ramasetu, the engineering marvel of a bridge Rama and *Vānarasena* built across the Indian Ocean from Dhanuṣkoṭi in Rameśwaram to Talaimannār in Śrilanka, to protect dharma by rescuing Sita from the clutches of Rāvaṇa. Kīṟakkarai is the source of *śankha* conch-shells and is the location for a flourishing industry supplying the shells. One Government report said that the annual turnover value of *śankha* is not less than Rupees 100 million. As I researched on this industrial complex, I could not find the link to the *śankha* bangle found in Mehergarh dated to 6500 BCE though we succeeded in convincing the Supreme Court that Ramasetu is a sacred temple, a world heritage. When we mooted the proposal to save this world heritage monument, 1.5 million people came from almost from every nook and corner of India and assembled in Rohini Park in New Delhi to give notice to the State that it is the State responsibility to protect this world heritage monument.

I cannot do better than Will and Ariel Durant who have narrated the *Story of Civilization* and Kapil Kapoor who has compiled the *Hindu Encyclopaedia*. Each of these works are in 11 volumes!

I abandoned this fascinating Kīṟakkarai track too because the narrative would have taken me far and wide into the Great Epic and everlasting message of Vālmīki's *Rāmāyaṇa* including the sundarakāṇḍa wherein Hanuman exclaims after finding Sita in Aśokavana: 'Draṣṭā Sita!' This episode is important because Hanuman thereafter deliberates on the choice of language to be used while narrating the story of Rama. 'Should it be Samskṛtam? Should it be Meluhha or Mleccha? If I speak in Samskṛtam, Sita may suspect that I am a spy sent by *Rāvaṇa*, since the asura was not merely a devotee of *Śiva* but an exponent of Samskṛtam.' Hanuman finally chooses Meluhha to narrate the story, starting from King Daśaratha in Ayodhya.

I finally decided to stay with the love story of Sagan Muṇḍa and Karmi Hatu.

I did not clutter the story with the accounts of how Sagan learnt the metallurgical alloying techniques and of how Sagan could distinguish zinc or tin or nickel minerals. Nor did I detail the electrum lead story for soma yajña though Lydians had used the gold-silver compound of electrum for making the early coins showing a one-horned young bull confronting a lion. Tamkarum 'merchant' (Phoenician) rebus: *ḍangar* 'bull' was confronting *ara* 'lion' (*ara* 'aryan' Akkadian) indicate the coalition of merchants and political governors in Lydia – an indication that the artisan-merchant's electrum coin was underwritten by the state.

"Syrians called Leo Aryo; the Jews, Arye; meaning a Lion. Ari or Aryeh, is the Hebrew for "lion", cognate with Akkadian aria, Aramaic arya. Aryeh in Sanskrit (a PIE, Proto-Indo-European, language) means "noble" and in Hebrew means "lion". Ari was used in Hebrew as an honorific for an important man. The Hebrew name Ari-el translates to "lion of God"...The original word in Vedic Language for Lion is 'Hari' which is phonically similar to ari."

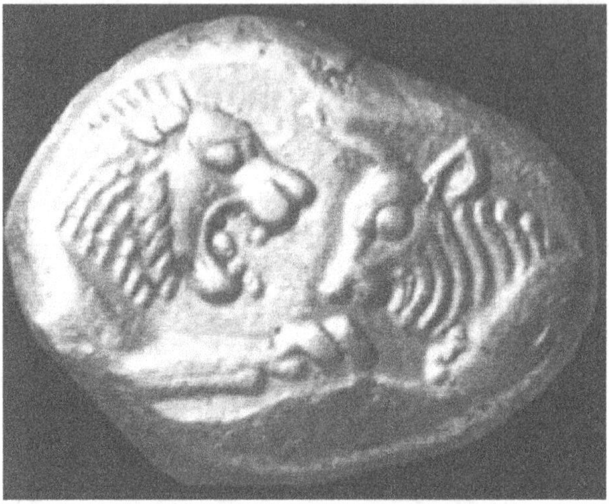

aruu = lion (As god of devastation, Nergal is called A-ri-a) (Akkadian) .

Rebus: Aru 'copper' (Akkadian) ara, era 'copper' (Pali. Pkt.)

Bull throwing lion. Green stone. Khafaje, Uruk (ca. 3200 - 3000 BC). Frankfort, Henri: Stratified Cylinder Seals from the Diyala Region. Oriental Institute Publications 72. Chicago: University of Chicago Press, no. 36.

Lydian electrum coin issued under the reign of Croesus (Fifth century BCE)

There are tomes written on the herbals used in the alchemical concoction to achieve a successful process of transmutation to create pure gold, starting with, say, copper. Newton had struggled with many alchemical techniques learned from ancient masters but did not provide any report similar to the ones which proved the existence of gravitational principle in physical phenomena.

There is a metaphysical principle of attraction which led the women depicted on Nausharo terracotta toys to choose sindhur, red vermilion as an ornamentation on the parting of the hair. I suppose I have conveyed the message of the stunning continuum of this practice of married women even today, as exemplified by Karmi Hatu decorating herself with sindhu on the parting of the hair. I chose to end the love story with this narrative because it is just amazing that despite millennia of earth's action transforming ancient settlements into mounds, the terracotta toys retained the red vermilion marks. I could not, till this day, fathom how the artisans could create such an indelible sindhur paste to anoint the toys.

This prologue will get too long if I try to document the civilization story of about 7 millennia concerning the lives of not less than one billion people today.

Sagan has already returned to his brass foundry to work with Karmi Hatu. He has a contractual deadline to meet to supply a large consignment of brass vessels of various shapes and sizes to a client in Iran. I often wonder how Sagan managed to strike such international supply contracts, despite competition from new technology stainless-steel automated, robot-driven vessel factories of Korea or Germany.

Sagan and Karmi prefer to continue the age-old traditional method of making brass vessels using the anvil and the mallet.

I also have a story to narrate about the ziggurat which lies under the unexcavated 'stupa' mound in Mohenjodaro overlooking what is referred to by archaeologists as 'The Great Bath'.. This would take me to the extraordinary life-story of mason Sugana and his wife Daskir.

Sugana and Daskir supervised the creation of sacred Wāvs, more breathtaking in splendor than 'the Great Bath', because they are temples celebrating water of life which is another phrase to explain the importance of Sarasvati in Indian civilization.

Sugana and Daskir have also been architects and builders of many temples as spectacular as the Sanchi Stupa.

I hope this narrative of how Sagan finds Sarasvati is enough for now as a curtain-raiser to record the maritime, cultural expeditions of. our ancestors, over long distances, hugging the coastline, along the Indian Ocean rim.

One hint should suffice: the batik design cloth in Indonesia is comparable to the work of cotton weavers of Gujarat. I do not know if the bronze work in Thailand of 6th millennium had any impact on the brass work of our ancestors and the manes adored and venerated by Sagan.and Karmi.

On one *śrāddham* day (day of remembering and paying homage to *pitṛ-s*) of their ancestors, Sagan and Karmi were pleasantly surprised to find a pair of *Anser indicus* nibbling at the wheat grains set out to dry in front of the courtyard in front of their brass foundry.

There is a painting by Ravi Varma which shows Rāvaṇa cutting the wings of Jaṭāyu.

So it is with this narrative which spans almost seven millennia of historical time-span and finally reporting that Sagan finds Sarasvati in Kāmyakavana, the way Hanuman finds Sita in Aśokavana as the rishis gathered in Naimiṣāraṇya to deliberate on the imperative of protecting dharma.

Sagan has outlined a schedule for the botanical expedition to Muztagh Ata, as a pair of hamsa, nibble at the wheat grains spread out to dry in front of the brass foundry of Sagan Munda and Karmi Hatu.

Fathomable are the mysteries of time as the epics remind us that what get categorized as myths are in fact, the truth, realized even by a judicial mind.

Mahākāla, inexorable, divine time, pauses, as the jury is still out.

Sagan and Karmi started moving to their brass foundry taking care not to disturb the pair of *Anser indicus* from their well-deserved break after a long journey across Mount Kailas. They recollected how Rama shed tears as he performed *śrāddham* ceremony for जटायुः Jaṭāyu who tried to rescue Sita from Rāvaṇa.

Sagan and Karmi felt overwhelmed by recollecting in tranquility the fond memories of such heroic fights of our ancestors to protect dharma. Prayers offered to the Akkadian morning sun are legacies to be cherished generation after generation.

About the author

Dr. S. Kalyanaraman is Director, Sarasvati Research Center, President, Ramasetu Protection Movement in India and BoD member of World Association for Vedic Studies. His research interests relate to rediscovery of Vedic Sarasvati River, roots of Hindu civilization, decoding of Indus Script, National Water Grid and creation of Indian Ocean Community. He has a Ph.D. in Public Administration from the University of the Philippines. He is a multi-lingual scholar versed in Tamil, Telugu, Kannada, Sanskrit, Hindi. He was a senior financial and IT executive in Asian Development Bank, Manila, Philippines and on Indian Railways. His 18 publications include: Indian Lexicon - a multilingual dictionary for over 25 Indian languages, Sarasvati in 15 volumes, Indian Alchemy - Soma in the Veda, Indus Script Cipher, Rastram, Indian Hieroglyphs, Harosheth Hagoyim, Indian Ocean Community, A Theory for Wealth of Nations. He is a recipient of many awards including Vakankar Award (2000), Shivananda Eminent Citizens' Award (2008) and Dr. Hedgewar Prajna Samman (2008).

Website: http://sites.google.com/site/kalyan97

About the book

Sagan in search of Sarasvati ends up in Muztagh Ata and encounters Chinese guards guarding the treasure of ancu. There were other seekers of ancu before him. He ends up in a bizarre court case in America. He visits Disney World Animal kingdom and takes a ride on the Kali River rapids. As the waters splash over him, he finds a friend on the ride. That friend from Kidarankondan guides him through the story of about seven millennia of people in search of ancu which is called amsu in an old human document called the Rigveda. Sagan finds the alchemical formula for making gold from mineral rocks of Muztagh Ata.

www.ingramcontent.com/pod-product-compliance
Lightning Source LLC
Chambersburg PA
CBHW061234170626
46809CB00007B/2670
* 9 7 8 0 9 8 2 8 9 7 1 9 5 *